Mating

Mating Heat - Book Three

By Laurann Dohner

Mating Brand by Laurann Dohner

Brand meets his dream girl in college—a half-human, half-snow leopard who's too human to shift. Werewolves and cats are natural enemies, but the power of their sexual chemistry overwhelms them. Charma steals his heart and makes him whole...until she abandons him, fracturing his world. Brand knows no woman can ever take her place. Though many seek his attention, he is cold and unattainable.

The love they share is soul deep but the fate of Charma's family lies in her hands. The memory of every heated touch will cut out both their hearts when she leaves, but to save them all, she must return to her pride...and to a man she loathes.

Now, after nine long years of desolation and heartbreak, Charma is back, risking her very life to warn Brand of an impending attack. He finally has her in his arms once more...and he'll do whatever it takes to never lose her again.

Dedication

To my hero—MrLaurann. Thank you for all your love and support. I couldn't do what I do without you.

Please note...

This book was originally put out a few years ago. It's a re-release. It's had some updated editing but I kept the original story intact.

Mating Heat Series

Mate Set

His Purrfect Mate

Mating Brand

Mating Brand

Copyright © April 2016

Editor: Kelli Collins

Cover Art: Dar Albert

ISBN: 978-1-944526-13-9

Prologue

The past

Hot, slick skin drew her mouth to his flat belly. The sheets had been kicked off. The window air conditioner droned softly from the other room but it wasn't a match for the sweltering heat of an early Texas summer.

Charma licked a bead of sweat just under Brand's belly button. She loved his taste, his scent—everything about him. He instantly responded. His cock stiffened, lengthened and proudly rose to full mast as a soft moan rumbled from his broad chest. She grinned and kissed the curve of his hip. His large hand brushed over her hair, then gripped her bare shoulder.

"Good morning," he rasped.

"Not quite but it's getting there." She lifted a little, gauged how awake he was, and opened her mouth again. Her tongue traced the underside of his shaft, making his cock twitch.

He raised his head to stare at her with passion-filled eyes. Their soft brown depths appeared more golden than chestnut when he woke. His nose flared and his body tensed. "You're going into heat."

She nodded, purposely breathing warm air on his sex as she spoke. "I know. I realized it when I woke. Should I take the pills? I need to start them right away to mute and control it, otherwise it's going to hit me full force in a matter of hours."

"Don't take them. We'll call in sick for the next few days." His hand caressed her shoulder. "I survived last month." His full, generous mouth curved into a grin. "I'm up for it."

She glanced down at the impressive evidence right in front of her mouth. "You certainly are."

He sat up. "Come here."

"I'm good where I am."

"You're better than good, but I also remember how aggressive you get." He chuckled. "And while I'm tough, I don't want your fangs giving me any accidental piercings."

"I won't bite."

"Hon, it's the only time of the month you grow fangs. I love you but I'm not risking it. I wouldn't be much good to you packed in ice until I heal tomorrow."

Charma pouted. "I want to taste you."

"Trust me. I'd love that too but you aren't in full control right now. Want me to show you the scars on my shoulder from last month?"

"I'm so sorry."

"It's okay. It's not a complaint. Stop apologizing. I like wearing your marks."

She sat up. "You could put a scar on me and I'd feel better."

Brand lunged, took her down flat on her back and pinned her under him. "It was an accident. You didn't mean to bite into me and I'd never mar your beautiful skin."

Her mood darkened. "I know."

"Hey." He adjusted over her until their noses touched and he stared into her eyes. "You're the one who won't mate with *me*. I want you to. That's the only way I'll ever sink my teeth into you."

She turned her head away to study the wall. Tears threatened to spill but she managed to blink most of them back. "You know I can't."

She could smell their pain as it filled the room, mingled, until she couldn't detect which one of them scented of it more strongly.

Brand suddenly rolled away and climbed off their bed. He stormed toward the door. "Take your pills."

"You're going to punish me?"

He stopped. She could stare at his big, sexy body all day. He didn't turn to look at her. "It's getting harder for me not to mate you. I think it's best if you take them to manage your heat. You'd hate me if I lost control." He left the room.

She lay there staring at the empty doorway long after she heard the shower come on. The urge to join him made her ache. It wasn't just because her body throbbed for sex or hormones now raged inside her. She loved Brand with all her heart and wanted nothing more than to mate with him. She just knew it could never happen.

Memories of four months ago filled her mind…

~ ~ ~ ~ ~

She was sitting in class listening to the history professor drone on and she barely heard the door open to admit someone who'd arrived late. She'd been tapping her thigh lightly with her thumb, trying to pay attention, but boredom had taken hold.

A scent filled her nose, nearly sending her into a panic.

She jerked her head to stare across the room at the really large, tall, black-haired male who took a seat. He didn't so much sit as plop down in an indolent sprawl. He had to be six feet four and about two hundred forty pounds. Most would assume, from his beefy, muscular body, that he belonged on the college football team. Charma knew better. The distinctive smell of werewolf assured her of the danger he posed.

It was clear the second he caught her scent. Instantly alert, he sat up straight. His head snapped in her direction and his dark gaze focused on her. Her fingers dug into her jeans as terror gripped her. The only things that kept her from bolting out of her seat to run for her life were the fifty students and the boring professor who were witnesses. He'd never attack her in front of humans. She was safer to remain still.

He frowned—then did the unexpected. He lifted a hand and gave her a small wave.

She gaped at him until a slow grin spread across his handsome face. Those soft brown eyes didn't flash a warning of impending attack. He winked instead before looking away to ignore her for the rest of the class.

Charma lingered inside the classroom after it ended, afraid to go outside in case he waited to drag her somewhere remote. There were plenty of places on the large Texas campus where no one would witness her death. Filled with dread, she finally headed for the door, knowing she couldn't hide there any longer.

He stood outside, just as she'd feared.

She stiffened, her heart pounded hard enough to cause pain, and she trembled. She knew she had no chance of surviving when he attacked.

"Calm down. I'm no threat." He frowned. "Damn, you're terrified. There's no reason to be."

She didn't believe him. They were natural enemies.

"I came to college to learn." His voice was pleasant, husky. "You know—meet new people, experience new things. You're the only person I've run into who is…" He paused and glanced around before meeting her gaze again. "Special."

She couldn't find her voice. It had to be a trap. He wanted to play with her, maybe lure her into a false sense of security and then strike for the fun of seeing the shock on her features before her death.

"I think we should leave bullshit family politics at home where they belong, don't you? We're just two college students right now. I swear I'm not going to hurt you." He drew in a deep breath through his nose. "Are you a panther?"

She still couldn't form words around the lump balled inside her throat. She shook her head instead. Her books felt extremely heavy, clutched in front of her chest to shield her heart if he decided to suddenly claw it out.

"I'm not familiar with your scent."

She cleared her throat. It took long seconds to work up the nerve to speak as she fought her instincts to flee. "I'm half human, half spotted leopard."

He grinned. "Really? I bet you're pretty when you shift. I mean," his smile faded, "you're pretty as a human but…you know what I mean."

"I can't shift." She wanted to kick herself for admitting that but her brain refused to work right. Terror made her blurt stupid things.

"Too human?"

"Please don't hurt me. I'll leave. I'll go to my dorm and can be gone in less than an hour. I don't own much so it won't take me long to pack."

"Aw, damn." His voice turned gruff. "Don't do that. What can I say or do to assure you that I'm no threat? I just waited around to make that clear and, um, I kind of hoped I could buy you coffee."

She gawked at him again.

"I'm used to being with a pack." A sheepish look crossed his features and he sighed, meeting her gaze again. "I'm lonely. We're surrounded by humans and I miss talking without always having to watch what I say. I was hoping we could hang out. I found a great spot where humans don't go. I guess if you can't shift, you wouldn't want to go running with me though."

He looked sincere and it stunned her. "I love to run anyway."

His expression brightened. "That's great. We could go together. Hell, I'm always worried about someone spotting me and calling animal control. They'd just think you were a woman out jogging with your big dog if you were with me." He laughed. "A *really* big dog that resembles a wolf, but most humans mistake me for a German Shepherd from a distance."

Charma started to relax. He wasn't growling at her or making threats. She was still breathing. All those things surprised her. "I haven't run into any other shifters."

"Most of us don't seem to go to college."

"True."

"I'm the only one in the history of my family. What about you?"

"The same."

"I really didn't mean to scare you. May I buy you coffee or dinner to make up for it? We should stick together. I bet you miss your pride."

She didn't dispute his assumption, though she disagreed. "You seriously want to spend time with me?"

"Yes." He moved slowly. "Those books look heavy. You're such a little thing. Allow me."

She didn't want to release them but she didn't have a choice when he gently pried them from her desperate hold. He watched her from his towering height.

"See? It's okay. I'm tame. Think of me as a big puppy."

He has to be kidding. The guy was a werewolf, one of the most feared shifter breeds ever born, and the enemy.

He offered her his arm next. "It's okay. I'm Brand Harris. What's your name?"

"Ch-Charma Heller."

"It's nice to meet you, Charma. There's a cafe around the corner. Lots of humans will be there if that makes you feel safer. It's okay." He held her gaze. "Really. I'm just lonely and thrilled to find someone else special I can talk to. I'd never hurt you."

"But we're natural enemies," she blurted, still not taking his arm.

"Says our parents." He made a point of peering around them. "I don't see them. Do you?" He flashed a friendly grin that once again made her notice his good looks. "I won't tell if you don't."

Indecision nagged at her but she finally reached for his arm. Her fingertips brushed warm, firm, tan skin. He didn't snarl or jerk away. She curled her fingers around his forearm as they walked together.

"It's a beautiful day, isn't it? I just arrived here after transferring from another school. It didn't work out there. I'm afraid a wolf running around California didn't go over well. I knew I had to take off when they started to pass out flyers to warn the students of a wild wolf."

A laugh escaped her. "Really?"

He actually blushed, his cheeks turning a rosy hue. "I messed up. Man, was my uncle pissed. How long have you been here?"

"This is my second year."

"What's your major?"

"I want to be a veterinarian."

He nodded. "I'm going for a business degree. So you got stuck with history too. Is that guy always so boring?"

"It was a required class, and yes, I'm afraid so. I play music inside my head just to stay awake." Charma completely relaxed…

~ ~ ~ ~ ~

14

Brand pulled her back to the present when he stepped into the bedroom with a towel slung low around his hips. He regarded Charma. "Did you take your pills?"

She crawled off the bed. "I'll do it now." She tried to pass him but his hand shot out to curl around her upper arm. She refused to look at him.

"I love you, and I know you love me too. I don't care how our families will react. I want to spend my life with you. I thought we started one together when we moved out of the dorms and rented this house. We're happy when we're not stressed about our future."

Charma turned her head to peer up at him. "I told you. My family made a bargain with the pride leader. I'm promised as mate to someone else and his family paid for college in exchange."

"I'll pay back every dime. My family has money."

"It's not that. It's about a promise."

"Paying for college isn't worth signing your life over to someone else." Anger deepened his voice to a snarl. "You don't want that jerk. You love *me*."

"I do." She turned into him, pressed her nose against his chest and inhaled his wonderful scent. "I love you so much." Her hot tears mingled with the chilled water droplets that remained on his skin from his cold shower. "I didn't have a choice. I would have been ordered to mate whomever the pride leader chose regardless.

But this way, I was able to postpone it and get an education first. He allowed it because they need a vet."

Brand released her arm to pull her tighter against him. "Hon, we can work this out somehow. I'll never let you go. We're mates already, even if we haven't cemented the bond yet."

She wished with her entire soul for that to be true. Fate had been cruel to her family. Brand didn't understand pride politics or the consequences if she didn't mate with Garrett Alter. She couldn't explain either. She was too afraid Brand would do something really insane to keep her. It would get him killed.

"Don't take the pills. Not even the ones to prevent pregnancy."

Her gaze shot up to lock with his. "You know I have to."

"Would it be so bad to have a baby with me?"

It would destroy her family. "It's probably not even possible. I've never heard of it happening. We're too different."

"Your human half could change that. We won't know unless we try."

"I just can't." Her voice broke and she pressed her face against his chest again, unable to witness the pained expression that twisted his features. "I do love you. Know that. No matter what happens in the future, you're the only man who will ever truly own me."

He snarled and suddenly jerked away. "Don't tell me that and then say I can't have you in the next breath. I need to go for a run." He spun, tore off his towel and stormed out of the room.

The front door slammed with enough force to shake the old cabin and Charma collapsed to her knees, tears sliding down her cheeks. Her obligation to her family was tearing them apart. She knew Brand would run himself into the ground to work out his frustration before he returned from the woods behind their home. She had at least an hour.

It took all her strength to rise to her feet. She couldn't destroy the man she loved, yet that was exactly what would happen if their bond grew stronger. One day she'd have to return home and leave him. If she left now, he'd only have a few months of memories to get past.

Her sobs carried her into the bathroom to take her pills. She nearly choked on the bitterness that carried them down her throat.

She gazed at her pale reflection in the mirror. Her blonde-and-brown-striped hair mocked her. Lots of humans had streaked hair, but hers was actually striped. It drew attention, and she'd been asked many times where she'd had it done. To avoid unwanted questions, she'd dyed it. But it was a trait she had stopped hiding at Brand's insistence, since hair dye made his nose itch. Her long hair flowed to her waist. She pulled her the wavy mass to the side and turned enough to see her back.

The dark spots along her lower spine were something she always hid beneath clothing or with her long hair. They were markings she'd been born with, ones that reminded her that no matter how much she wished she could change her heritage, it

17

would never happen. They kept her from passing as human…but the shifter world was destroying her one day at a time.

Her gaze lifted to stare into her blue-and-yellow eyes. The yellow flecks in her irises seemed more pronounced from crying. She reached for the contacts that hid that uniqueness from humans and made her appear totally normal.

There was only one thing to do. She had to leave Brand to spare him more pain. She loved him too much to be selfish. More tears spilled until they blinded her but she moved on wooden legs to pack her things. She needed to be gone before he returned.

She threw back her head in anguish and stifled a scream.

* * * * *

Brand howled with grief after a quick search of their home.

Charma's clothes no longer hung in the closet with his and her car wasn't parked next to his truck when he rushed outside. He panted, sniffing. No gas exhaust hung in the air. She'd been gone for at least half an hour or he'd have smelled the engine still.

He spun and went back inside the house. *NO!* He couldn't bear the thought of never seeing her again. The first shirt he grabbed ripped in his hands, making him aware that his claws were out.

"Fuck!" He had to pull himself together enough to get dressed without damaging everything he owned. He didn't bother to put on shoes, just jeans and a T-shirt. He snagged his keys and rushed out the door.

Please break down, he prayed as he threw his truck in reverse and nearly slammed the tailgate into a tree in his rush. Her car was an old clunker and had an oil leak he'd planned to fix but she hardly drove it. He threw the vehicle in drive and punched it. The ass end slid on the grass as he took off.

His frantic gaze scanned the road ahead as he took the curves far too fast for safety. He only slowed when he entered town, afraid the cops would pull him over. He couldn't waste time getting a ticket.

Where would she go? She didn't have many friends. The fear of discovery was too great. The college girls loved to go swimming at the river but his Charma was afraid they'd see the faint spots trailing down her spine. He'd assured her a hundred times she could say they were tattoos but she didn't like to lie.

Oh, baby. Where are you? Don't do this. Don't leave me. He drove past one of the dorms, searching for her car. It wasn't there. Within ten minutes he was sure she hadn't gone to crash with Dina or Barbara.

Panic set in. She might have left town altogether. He made his way to the main highway and checked out the gas station. She wasn't there but he stopped anyway and went inside.

The guy behind the counter frowned at his bare feet. "No shoes, no service."

Brand wanted to snarl but terrifying the clerk wouldn't be to his advantage. "I'm sorry. My girlfriend is missing and I'm worried something has happened to her. She drives an old rusted ford."

"Ah. The one with the cool two-toned hair down to her butt?"

"Yeah. Charma. Have you seen her lately?"

The clerk nodded. "She was in here about forty minutes ago. She filled up her tank and bought a few candy bars."

Filled the tank. He felt as if someone had punched him in the gut. "Did she say where she was heading? Ask for directions? That car breaks down."

Suspicion narrowed the clerk's eyes. "You guys have a fight?"

Brand reached up and ran his fingers through his hair in frustration. "Yeah. It was stupid and I stormed out. I came back and she was gone. Please tell me what you know. I can't lose her."

"I don't blame you. She's a babe."

It took a lot of control for Brand not to lunge over the counter and tear the asshole's throat out for noticing that about his woman. "Did she say where she was heading? I have to find her and tell her I'm sorry."

The clerk hesitated. "No but I saw her get on the freeway. She went east."

"Thank you!" Brand rushed outside, realizing he'd left his door open and the motor running. He jumped in the truck and drove like a madman, pushing the engine to the limit as he surpassed speeds of over a hundred and ten, weaving through traffic, searching for her car. His enhanced reflexes saved him from crashing a few times. The hope of catching up to her lasted until he reached a four-way split on the freeway.

He tried to feel out her presence, using his senses to see if he could track her, but nothing happened. "NO!"

He checked his mirrors and crossed four lanes, only to slam on the brakes along the shoulder. He got out and sniffed the air, hoping to catch her scent. It was a long shot but he was desperate. Exhaust from the traffic choked him and he dropped to his knees beside the open truck door. He bellowed, "CHARMA!"

Chapter One

Nine years later

"Charma?"

She turned her head to peer at her sister. "What, Bree?"

"You've got that sad look on your face again. I thought we were past this. You can't stop me from growing up. I'm an adult."

"I'm fine." She lied with ease, something she'd spent years perfecting. "I was just thinking about Dad."

"Oh." Her younger sister reached out to squeeze her hand. "He's going to do great. You heard Garrett. This won't be his first surgery or his last. This new procedure will help him get more use out of his leg so he doesn't have to keep depending on the cane."

She had to turn away to hide the anger. "Yes. I heard him."

"Garrett is *so* hot. I envy you. I want to find a mate as fine as him now that I'm of age."

A shudder ran down Charma's spine. "I hope not," she whispered.

"I heard that." Her sister snagged her arm and spun her around.

Charma couldn't suppress a gasp of pain. Bree frowned and her gaze lowered from her sister's face to her arm. "What's wrong with you?"

"Nothing."

"Let me see your arm. Pull up your sleeve."

"It's nothing. I bumped it last night." She eased out of her sister's hold and forced another smile. "What dress do you want to buy? This is your party. Garrett said to spare no expense."

"Char," Bree's green eyes narrowed. "Show me your fucking arm."

"Such language from a teenager. Is that what they taught you in school?"

Her sister hissed. "Show me your arm. You have a lot of *accidents*. Is…" Her sister paled. "Does Garrett hit you? We had an assembly at school about domestic abuse before graduation and I'm doing the math. I don't like what I'm coming up with."

"Of course not."

"Then show me this bump."

"It's just a bruise." Charma tried to turn away but her sister moved to block her.

"Show it to me now or I'll assume your mate is hurting you."

"Mind your own business."

Her sister paled even more. "Oh. My. God!" Tears filled her eyes. "I knew it wasn't a love match, but shit. Do our parents know?"

Charma glanced around the dress shop. "Lower your voice."

23

"Your mate is abusing you and you're worried about what someone else will think? You're not someone who would take that bullshit!"

She gripped her sister's hand and tugged her inside the dressing room, alert for any sign of someone approaching. The flimsy door sealed them into the small area.

"You've got to calm down."

"No! I'm going to tell his father. I'm going to tell everyone!"

"No," Charma hissed. "Listen to me. You're old enough to know the truth since you stumbled on to it. Everyone in the pride has known for years about what's been going on. It's not a secret that I was forced to mate with Garrett. He's a cold bastard but he's the future pride leader. His father paid for me to go to college after he decided I was the one he wanted."

"But you never finished. You came home. You couldn't owe that much money, and that's *no* reason to agree to mate someone."

"Dad was crippled and mom was badly scarred. He could never shift again after their car accident. He couldn't protect our family so he made a deal. He asked Garrett's dad to allow me to go to college first. I had to submit to the mating after I came home, regardless of whether I'd finished or not. Do you understand?"

"No, I don't. Why would you agree to that bullshit? You could have taken a loan or something. Gotten a scholarship. How could you sell yourself that way?"

"It wasn't about money." Charma took a deep breath. "Listen to me closely, Bree. You don't walk away from a pride unless you're prepared to die. And I don't mean just one member, but the entire family. Weakness is not tolerated. That was the deal. I agreed to the terms to keep us safe. *All of us.* Dad was deemed useless after that accident, unworthy of living."

Horror crept across her sister's features and she leaned heavily against the wall. "Are you saying if you hadn't mated with that prick...?" Her voice trailed off.

"Yes. Percy would have killed Dad, and if he had, Mom's scars and her surgery would have made it impossible for her to mate with someone else to protect us. She can't have more children and what male in a pride wants a scarred-up human woman who's unable to give him offspring? It's unfair but it's reality. You know Percy is ruthless—and his son takes after him. I wanted nothing to do with Garrett, then the car accident happened, and they had the perfect leverage to get their way. I had no choice, and neither did our parents."

"You could have run away." Bree nodded frantically. "We could have fled as a family."

"Do you think I didn't consider that? Where would we have gone? We'd have been inside werewolf territory if we'd gone anywhere other than pride lands. We had to avoid other prides because death is basic protocol when dealing with the weak. They'd have killed our parents and the worst would have happened."

"What could be worse than death?"

Charma hesitated. "Some prides—not ours, but a lot of them—use half-blooded females for breeders to increase their numbers. They won't mate with them but instead force them to accept any male who wants to impregnate them. Many of them at once, if she can't shift, since ones like us can breed litters. We wouldn't have been given a choice and they don't even allow you to keep your babies. They're given to others to raise."

"No." Bree noticeably paled, horror reflected in her wide eyes. "That's barbaric."

"Yes. You've been shielded from a lot of harsh truths, Bree. Some other pride wouldn't have waited until you turned eighteen or finished high school before that hellish life was shoved on you. You get to pick your mate now, because we're in a pride that doesn't condone that kind of shit. Only one man will touch you and your babies are your own to keep. Percy may be a cruel asshole but he abides by the old traditions."

Anger showed on Bree's face. "That doesn't change the fact that we can't stay here. Your mate is abusing you."

Charma wanted to hug her sister but refrained. "You're safe in our pride. Megan mated a good male and *his* family protects ours now. I'm just trapped because I belong to Garrett."

"You should flee."

"Where would I go?" Her shoulders straightened. "Do you think I haven't considered that? At least here, only one male abuses me and I get to see my family. It's not so bad, Bree. Really. Garrett and I avoid each other as much as possible and he's seeing other women who take care of his physical needs."

Shock widened her sister's eyes. "But you're mated!"

"Lower your voice!"

"He can't cheat on you," Bree hissed. "He's your mate. It's unnatural."

"So is a loveless mating. It happens sometimes though. I'm actually grateful he seeks other women. I keep praying he gets one of them pregnant and sets me aside. It's forbidden for me to leave him."

"He'll kill you. That's the only way a mating ends."

"He's been ordered by his father to keep me alive. He'll shun me, toss me out of his home, and mate the new female as though I'd died if he impregnates one of them. It's rare but it's happened. Percy told him to keep me as a mate for now because he doesn't want to make waves unless he can justify Garrett setting me aside." She absently rubbed her sore arm. "That's why he occasionally attacks me. He's just angry that he can't snap my neck. Shunning a sterile mate for a woman who can breed is acceptable to the pride."

"You're sterile? Oh my god." Tears filled her sister's eyes. "I'm so sorry. Are you sure?"

A hum startled Charma and she reached inside her purse to withdraw her cell phone. The timing was perfect, saving her from answering the question. She read the display. "Quiet. It's Percy." She answered. "Hello."

"Get back here. We have a situation," Percy snapped. "Where are you?"

"I'm a few minutes away. I'm coming back to the office now."

"Hurry." He hung up.

Charma studied her younger sister. "The important thing is, what I did safeguarded our family long enough for Megan to mature and find her own mate. Our family is protected now. That alone has been worth everything. I have to go."

"But—"

"I love you. Buy something nice for your party but not too revealing." She shoved cash at her sister and yanked open the door to flee.

"Charma?"

She paused, turning back to hold her sister's gaze. "What?"

"You shouldn't take that shit from Garrett."

"I know but I don't have a choice. Life isn't always fair, hon."

"You mean like this party? It's so old-fashioned to dress me up as if I'm a piece of meat to shove in front of all the guys until one of them wants to bite." Her voice lowered. "Why do they make us find mates so fast?"

"It's because of the heat. They want women mated and settled so there's little to no risk of fights. Some guys kill each other if they want a woman bad enough when she's in heat. Percy also doesn't ever want children born outside matehood. He thinks it undermines our society."

"Haven't they heard of birth control? I have." Her voice lowered. "Sex toys handle the heat just fine. It doesn't mean I have to let any jerk nail me because it's that time of the month."

"I don't agree with these parties either but I can't do anything to stop it. It's ultimately up to you whom you decide to mate. Remember that, and don't allow Percy or anyone else to push you at someone you don't love. Trust me when I tell you that a loveless mating is the worst. I have to go."

She rushed outside and wasted no time reaching the edge of town, where the pride kept an office. She knew when she stepped inside the building that something serious had happened. Nine of the strongest fighters were clustered in the waiting room, all grim-faced. The door on the other side of the room jerked open.

Percy Alter stepped out of his private office. To Charma, he was the epitome of hypocrisy. He may have appeared to be in his mid-forties, handsome and kind, but looks were deceiving. He neared eighty in real years, the good-looking face masked an ugly beast, and he relished ruling his pride with sheer cruelty.

"One of the prides has been attacked by werewolves." Rage sparked in his green eyes. "The pride leader lost two of his sons, as well as an unknown number of males. The joining call has been accepted."

Fear instantly gripped Charma. She knew what that meant. The pride council had ordered some of the larger prides to send males to assist a smaller group in a fight. They were at war.

Had the werewolves finally decided to wipe out all cat-shifter prides? It had been a threat hanging over them for all of history.

"You nine will go to represent our pride. At least thirty males in all will be sent to the pride in need. That should immediately wipe out the threat." Percy turned his focus on Charma. "Turn on that damn computer and make yourself useful. Pull up the information. The council sent pictures of the targets."

She rushed to her desk, tried to ignore her trembling hands and sat heavily on her chair. The computer had been left on but the pride leader didn't know how to work one or even turn on a monitor. Most of the pride males didn't excel in in school except for sports. Gaining an education wasn't something they did beyond high school since it elevated the risk of discovery of what they truly were. Charma had been the exception.

Of course, she'd never finished college. Charma had been forced to be the leader's secretary after she'd returned home from Texas. He depended on her skills, which afforded her some protection from his son.

The email waited in the pride's inbox and she turned the monitor until everyone in the room could see it. She gripped the mouse, opened the file, and pictures loaded on the screen. She kept her attention on Percy as he stomped forward.

"There's the enemy. They are vicious killers."

When the outer door opened to admit her mate, the scent of him made her cringe. She avoided glancing his way.

"Father, what's happened?"

"A joining has been called by the council. You didn't need to come, Garrett. I'm not sending you. You're too valuable for me to risk losing in this battle."

Charma fought to suppress her disappointment. For an instant she'd hoped her mate might leave and she'd contemplated the idea of him being killed. That would have been too neat, too wonderful, and good things never happened to her. She turned her focus to the monitor instead, the angle of the screen just out of her view until she pushed her chair over enough to see it more clearly.

The first face she glimpsed was of a young, handsome blond male. Under his picture a name—Yon—had been typed in bold white letters.

The next picture flashed. The guy had black hair and intense dark eyes. Another good-looking wolf who seemed to be in his forties. Alpha Elroy. He didn't appear mean but her gaze shifted to Percy. *He doesn't either but...total nightmare.*

"That's the pack next to the Bowmont pride, right?" Randy, the lead enforcer, stepped closer. "I've heard of them. They're known to be pretty tough fighters and very territorial."

"That's them," Percy snarled. "They won't be much of anything for long. Charma? Don't just sit there. Get up and bring me food. I'm hungry."

She rose from her chair and entered the kitchenette. Not only did she run all the pride leader's errands and play secretary, but he'd made her his personal servant and whipping girl as well.

Her teeth clenched as she forced her anger down. They'd smell it if she didn't quickly get control of her emotions. Percy would strike her in front of the enforcers and her mate, something she'd do anything to avoid. She knew how much Garrett would enjoy seeing her punished.

She turned. "What would you like for lunch?"

The pride leader waved a dismissive hand. "I don't give a damn. Just feed me."

Motion drew her attention and she met the glare of her mate. Her spine stiffened at the malevolent look he directed her way. He stalked closer to his father. "Feed me as well. You can rub my feet after you're done."

Hatred warmed her entire body. He'd make her drop to her knees in front of everyone just to humiliate her. He'd beat her if she refused. Charma found herself wishing she had some poison to sprinkle over anything she fed Garrett. His sense of smell wouldn't allow that fantasy to ever become a reality.

He could do worse. She just spun away and jerked open the small fridge in the corner of the kitchenette. She'd never forgive Garrett for even a tenth of the horrible things he'd done to her over the years. He really enjoyed humiliating her in front of the enforcers and his father whenever possible.

She quickly made a stack of sandwiches and took some to Percy first. He didn't thank her, never had, and she'd fall over in shock if he ever did. She glanced at the monitor while she waited for him to take the plate.

The face on the screen made her freeze.

No. It can't be. Her gaze lowered to the name under the picture. *Brand!*

"My food," Garrett growled. "Now."

She automatically responded to years of taking his commands and twisted away from the sight that shocked her to the core and rushed back to grab the second plate. She avoided looking directly at him as she handed the food to Garrett. He accepted it with one hand and painfully gripped her shoulder with the other.

"Rub my feet."

"Not now," Percy snapped. "Make her do that later. I want her to print out four copies of the map they sent. She takes *my* orders while she's here."

"She's *my* mate!" Garrett's grip tightened until she whimpered from pain.

"Let her go!" Percy roared.

Garrett shoved her away and Charma stumbled to her chair. All the men followed Percy into his office and the door slammed. She lunged for the monitor to twist it her way. She quickly halted the flashing pictures to back them up a few frames and stared at a face she'd never thought she'd see again.

Brand had grown out his hair. Small lines bracketed his mouth and marked the outer edges of his sexy eyes as he smiled at whoever had taken the picture. He wore faded blue jeans and a navy tank top. She stared at his buff, tanned arms, remembering the feel of them wrapped around her. Her heart lurched.

He's in danger.

That thought sank in.

"Where are those damn maps?" Percy roared from the other room.

"The internet is really slow," she lied. "I'm downloading them."

"Hurry up," her pride leader demanded.

Her fingers flew over the keyboard as she frantically worked. Percy had never been known for his patience. It took only a few minutes to pull up a map, open it in a photo program, scramble the names of a few towns to make certain the attack party got lost if

34

they followed the driving directions she changed, then quickly printed out the copies. Her knees felt weak as she entered the office.

Her mate stuck out his foot as she walked toward the desk, tripped her, and she slammed into the floor on her belly at the feet of two of the enforcers. She pushed up to her hands and knees to shove the papers on Percy's desk.

A firm hand gripped her elbow to assist her to stand. She shot a grateful look at Randy. He didn't release her though. He frowned as he drew air into his nose. His gaze left her to stare at Garrett.

"Your mark is fading from her. It's faint."

"So?"

"So it's my job to keep the peace, and some of the males might go after your mate unless you cover her again with your mark. I can barely pick it up. I don't want to have to bury any of our members when you tear them apart."

Garrett snorted. "Nobody would want her. She's useless. She's infertile, a rotten lay, and unless I'm smacking her, she doesn't even move while I'm nailing her."

Charma wished the floor would open up under her feet. She could sense every male watching her. She should have known her mate would retaliate for what had occurred the night before when he'd entered her area of their home in a drunken stupor. It had been one of the rare occurrences when he'd sought her out, but she'd spurned his sexual advances.

35

"One of the pride will attempt to fuck her if you don't strengthen your scent," Randy persisted. "You might not think so, but she's very pretty."

"I don't care what happens to her."

Randy released her arm. "You're saying you don't give a damn if other pride go after her? She's only half-blooded. She won't be able to fight them off."

"Nope. Hell, you want her, fuck her right here. You'll be disappointed if you think it's going to be any good. Any of you can have her if you want. Bend her over the nearest chair if you're in the mood."

Horror gripped Charma. Her gaze lifted to Randy, praying he'd protect her even if her mate wouldn't. Interest sparked in his green eyes and he licked his lips.

"You sure? I've always wondered what it would be like to have her."

"I'd find it amusing as hell." Garrett chuckled. "Go for it. Just be rough."

"Not inside my office, on my furniture." Percy sighed. "Do it on *your* time. Right now, she's got shit to do other than amusing your friends, son." Percy waved her off. "Go. We're busy. Tomorrow night, we're declaring war on those damn werewolves."

She fled toward the door, wanted to escape, but paused to address her pride leader. "Your dry cleaning is ready. Should I pick it up now or wait until later?"

"Go but come right back. We're going to need coffee soon while we plan the attack."

She backed up, avoiding Garrett and the other men, who watched her with way too much interest. As soon as she reached her desk, she grabbed her purse and car keys before bolting from the office.

There was no going back once she left town. The Pride would kill her for betraying them, but it beat sticking around waiting for Garrett to allow the enforcers to have her. He would do it. Her mate was a total bastard. The fact that he would outlive her was the only regret she suffered as she climbed into her car.

Within twenty minutes, Percy would figure out she hadn't returned and send some of the enforcers to hunt her. Within two hours, they'd realize she wasn't within pride lands.

She rolled down her window and reached inside her purse. She glanced at the phone, tempted to call her family to say goodbye, but rejected the idea. Her parents would demand she stay. She also didn't want to have to explain to her siblings exactly how bad life had gotten for her. They'd be safe from retaliation, since her sister had mated with the alpha's son from another pack. It would be an offense to that pride if Percy or Garrett hurt Megan's family.

Charma pitched the device out the window. She could be traced by it, and she didn't want to weaken her resolve to do the right thing. Calling one of her siblings made that a real possibility.

Fear nearly overwhelmed her but a memory surfaced. The image of Brand smiling at her from across a candlelit table on their first official date soothed her. *I can do this. For him.*

* * * * *

Brand jerked awake, panting from the nightmare of reliving the worst day of his life—the day Charma had fled. He was twisted up in the bedding, sweat covered his body and his dick was rock hard. He glanced down at the tented sheet.

"Yeah, I know who you want, but she's not here."

He sat up, shoved the sheet away, and stood. His skin was overheated, his gums ached and he knew why. "I hate this time of year. Goddamn mating heat."

It disgusted him that his evening would consist of porn flicks and lotion. He had stopped going to the pack runnings once he realized that he'd never find a mate there. He had tried it for years, hopeful someone would make him forget that she-cat, but eventually acceptance had settled in. The random sex gave him a break from routine but after a while, even that bored him. It just wasn't worth the bullshit.

The phone rang and he stared at it. He wasn't on duty until tomorrow. The answering machine picked up after three rings.

"Hello? Brand? It's Peggy!" The annoying voice grated on his nerves. "You haven't called me back. I'm going to the running in an hour and wanted to make sure you know where to meet me." She giggled, sounding like a teenager instead of a thirty-year-old mother of nine. "I'm really excited. Don't be late. I don't want to have to fight off other males if they find me first. You're the one I want. I'll be at the creek where the white rocks are, near the waterfall." She hung up.

The woman had lost her mate and was looking to make him the father and provider for her family. She chased him often but he wasn't having any of it. She only wanted him for his home and money and wasn't even polite enough to lie about it. He had to give her credit for honesty, at least. She'd told him flat out why she'd chosen him. She'd loved her mate but figured Brand would welcome a relationship where no emotions were involved. She had also tired of dealing with nine kids alone.

"Not happening," he groaned. "I might not be the friendliest bastard but I'm not desperate either."

The phone rang as he reached the master bathroom to take his shower. He paused and waited as the answering machine clicked on.

"Brand? It's Melissa." The woman paused. "The guy I agreed to hook up with chose another bitch who wiggled her tail at him." Anger deepened her voice. "I thought since that fell through, maybe you and I could get together instead. I figured you'd still be

39

available. I hate this time of year, don't you? Hey, it beats batteries, right? Give me a call back soon or I'll find someone else." She hung up.

"Right," he muttered. "I'm so flattered to be your second choice and better than a vibrator. You thinking of some other guy while I'm nailing you is such a turn-on." He snorted. "I'll pass."

He flicked on the bathroom light and quickly shoved down his sweat pants. He twisted the lever to cold, hoping the spray sluicing down his body would cool his heated blood.

He glanced down at his dick, which refused to soften, and clenched his teeth. He hated mating heat, detested that once a year, he kept a constant boner and wished he were a woman. They had it slightly easier. They suffered severe horniness but it wasn't painful, didn't drive them out their minds or make them turn into pitiful creatures who jacked off frantically to anything flashing skin, even on television.

He shook his head and tipped it back under the icy blast of water. He knew it wouldn't work. His cock seemed to have a pulse and a growl tore from his throat. His balls ached too. He quickly washed his hair, turned off the water, and snatched a towel off the rack.

The phone rang again. He tilted his head as he dried off while avoiding his middle and perked up when his ex-girlfriend's voice met his ears. Hope soared that she might want to spend time with him. She was pretty, made him laugh, and he'd had a good time

40

with her until she'd cheated on him with another wolf and insisted that he was to blame. It wasn't a match made in heaven but he'd take it during mating heat.

"Hey, stranger. Um, this may be a bit awkward but I know you're still single. My grandma hasn't gone through menopause yet and, well, hell…you've got to be hard up, since most know to avoid you because you're not looking for anything lasting. She's been reading these books about cougars. That's what they call older women who fuck younger guys. She always thought you were hot and wondered what it would be like having a young stud go after her again. She was totally excited when I told her how good in bed you are. I told her you'd be flattered she wants you and you'd go for it. You remember where she lives, right? Just go over there and she'll take care of you during the heat. You're welcome!"

Brand dropped the towel, horrified. A memory of Jackie's grandmother flashed through his mind. The woman had to be past a hundred and actually *looked* like someone's grandma. She had baked cookies for the occasion when she'd met her granddaughter's "nice young man". He remembered her using a walker to get around after breaking her hip when she'd lost a fight with a bear she'd encountered in the woods.

The idea of doing her made his cock lower slightly. He peered down. It remained hard but he could see a little difference…until it perked right back up.

"Goddamn it!" he roared. "I'd rather hump a pillow. I *hate* mating heat!"

He snarled as he stormed to the nightstand and yanked the drawer open in his haste to grab a bottle of lotion. "Her *grandmother*. Shit. That's just mean." The memory of the older woman flashed again and he paused.

"No damn way." He'd rather meet up with Peggy, though he was certain she would try to get him hot enough to lose his mind and bite her to seal the mating deal. She'd own him then, her and the nine pups he'd have to care for. He'd be mated and destined to be nothing more than her checkbook and pup wrangler. "I hate my damn life."

He threw his ass on the bed, opened the lotion bottle and was about to tip it to pour a generous amount into his palm when the phone rang again. He paused. He needed to ease the tension inside his body. He had to get off to stop the pain that had become nearly unbearable.

"Who's next? Someone trying to shove their three-legged cousin at me? Maybe someone's going to ask me if I'm hard up enough to do barn animals?"

"Brand? Pick up now," Jeff ordered. "We have a situation."

He lunged across the bed, dropping the lotion. He jerked the phone from the cradle to shove it against his ear. "What's wrong?"

Something bad had to have happened for an enforcer on duty to call.

"You're not going to believe this if I tell you. Just get your ass into town."

"Where?"

"Oh, you can't miss it. Just hurry. I'm trying to hold them back but they're going to tear the damn car apart if they get past me."

"What—"

"Just get here! This—" Howls drowned out anything else Jeff may have said before the connection died.

Brand hung up and ran to the dresser, cursing a blue streak as he tried to zip his jeans over his swollen cock. He grinned though. If he couldn't fuck, fighting would work. He grinned, though, as excitement hit him. If he couldn't fuck...

Chapter Two

Charma whimpered and climbed into the back of the car. She'd hoped having the windows up would mask her scent when she'd driven into town, but she'd been wrong. The driver's window hadn't smashed in yet but it had spiderwebbed enough to terrify her. That had motivated her to scramble over the seats.

The entire vehicle shook when someone jumped on the hood. A terrifying howl hurt her ears and a boot slammed into the windshield. The safety glass held but the window cracked in at least a two-foot diameter. Someone else grabbed the passenger door and jerked hard enough to make the car sway. The lock held but the male snarled, enraged that he couldn't get to her.

"Back off," another male yelled. "That's an order! Damn it, get off the car. Back away."

Bodies nearly blocked out the streetlights as they converged and she knew she only had moments before they managed to tear through some part of the car to reach her. They weren't going to allow her to talk. She'd hoped they'd just ask her why she'd trespassed into their territory.

That had been the plan, which had gone terribly awry as soon as she'd turned off the engine. In what seemed like mere seconds, men had rushed at her from all directions.

They rocked the car until it made her slip on the seat. She fell over onto her side, drew her knees up to her chest and huddled into a tight ball. Howls and snarls were nearly deafening. She covered her ears, squeezed her eyes shut, and her heart raced.

She knew death would come soon. Still, it had to be better than what her mate planned for her. He'd tried to destroy her soul a day at a time. Now he'd told the enforcers they could take her body if they wanted. She'd rather be killed by werewolves. They were brutal but swift death-bringers.

Glass shattered and rained down over her. She screamed when a hand fisted her hair and pulled. Her body slid closer to the destroyed window and pain stabbed her. The one who held her howled, so close it was deafening, and she screamed again.

The hand suddenly released her hair.

"Enough!" a horrifyingly deep voice roared. "Do you want to die?"

The male who spoke wasn't human. His voice was so affected she could barely understand the words.

"That's a *female*, damn it! Who said you could kill her?"

"It's a damn cat," another deep voice snarled. "She asked for it."

Charma lifted her head and peeked up. She'd been pulled all the way to the door until her head actually touched the armrest. She stared at a broad-backed male wearing a gray sweater. He leaned against the opening, covering it with his body to prevent anyone from grabbing her again.

"We kill stinking cats where I come from!" a werewolf shouted.

The guy against the door emitted a vicious sound. "You're in Harris Pack territory now. You're a visitor, and you will follow our laws. We don't kill females, even she-cats. Leave if you don't like it!"

The guy protecting the opening moved enough for Charma to see more of him. He'd kept his human form but some hair covered the backs of his hands. Fresh blood dripped from the spiky points of his extended claws. They appeared to be razor sharp and deadly.

She inhaled but there were so many angry wolves surrounding her car that she couldn't smell anything other than overpowering werewolf scent. It nearly overwhelmed her and her heart raced faster. She almost screamed at the sheer horror of being completely surrounded by the enemy but another whimper escaped instead.

"Go into the woods," the man leaning against the car demanded in a harsh growl. "*Now*. You'll get worse than the ones on the ground if you stay. My cousins are on their way. If I could take down seven of you, think about what *they* can do. They're more alpha-blooded than I am."

Charma panted. The smell of the werewolves had become so dense she could taste it. Her gaze locked on the gray sweater of the male who had stopped the attack. She prayed he wasn't sending the rest of his pack away to slaughter her himself. She just needed a chance to talk. She would warn them of the pride males who planned to declare war and hopefully they'd be grateful enough for the warning that they might spare her life.

Part of her longed to use Brand's name but she didn't want his pack to turn on him. She'd rather them not know they'd ever met. She'd come to save him, not put him in danger from his own kind. She'd let him down once but she'd make it right; owed him that and so much more.

She wondered if he'd mated…

Of course he has. The image of his handsome face still haunted her. *Women would have chased him in droves. Or in a pack,* she corrected. It still hurt to imagine some woman curled against his side every night. *Kissing him. Running her hands through his silky hair and —*

Stop! Don't go there.

"I'm sorry," a new voice panted. "I tried to hold them back but there were too many. Thanks for coming so fast, man. Is she alive?"

The male against the door shook his hands, blood flying off them, and his claws slowly retracted. "Yeah." His voice still came out as a snarl. "I hear her breathing. I need to calm down for a minute."

"No shit. Wow. I thought only Rave could fight like that. It was impressive."

47

"Who do you think he learned to fight with growing up, Jeff?" The voice lowered a little, changing from snarly to gruff. "We're damn close, and trained with each other as if we were brothers."

Jeff cleared his throat. "Do you think that's Shannon's mom? I figured that's who had come here when I smelled she-cat. She probably wants to meet her son-by-mate. I tried to call Anton but he didn't pick up."

"Shannon's mother is human. It was her father who was half shifter. He's dead and she's estranged from his family." The voice toned down more. "How's my face? Still hairy? I don't want to scare her."

"You're good. I doubt after what just happened that anything is going to calm her."

"Drag the injured away before any humans happen along. It's after nine. Most of the townspeople stay in after dark at this time of year but it would be our luck if someone happened to run out of milk or something. I also heard we have some tourists parked outside of town. They tried to stay at the hotel but Marcy told them it was booked."

"Got it. A few more enforcers will be here at any second. We'll clean up this mess and tend to the wounded. They're lucky you allowed them to live."

A loud sigh sounded. "Are my cousins on the way or did I just lie?"

"Rave is coming. Von didn't pick up but he's patrolling the woods. I figured he didn't get cell service. Grady didn't pick up, so I'm sure *he's* having sex. Both he and Anton turn their phones off when they're bonding with their mates. I didn't bother calling Braden. At his age, he's probably out of his head with the heat, and I know he's staying with you. I thought you'd bring him, though, if you needed help."

"It sounded urgent. I didn't waste time to grab him. Go on. I'll deal with this."

A rumbling sound fractured the evening and Charma swallowed hard. The distinctive noise grew louder until the motorcycle engine cut off. "Shit. Looks as though I missed some good times. Is any of that blood on the ground yours?"

"Nope," the guy in the sweater muttered.

"I smell blood, lust, anger…and is that a she-cat? That's not Shannon. I'll never forget the scent of her in heat for as long as I live." The new guy chuckled. "I doubt any of us ever will. Damn. I envy my big bro."

"Rave, not cool. He'd be seriously angry if he heard you say that."

"I don't see him here, do you? Is she okay? Do you want to move and allow me to check on her? I'm cool with kittens."

"Go for it. I'm still trying to calm down."

"I can see *and* hear that. Your voice is all screwed up. Snarl much lately to scare off the weaker?"

"Shut the hell up and deal with her before more of them sniff her out. She probably took a wrong turn."

The car swayed when the guy pushed off it to walk away. Charma sat up on the seat to gaze out the busted window. Shattered glass slid to the floor when she moved. A big leather-jacketed werewolf strode forward but paused a few feet away. He crouched down to peer back at her. His shaggy black hair was familiar and a pair of dark brown eyes met hers.

"Hi there. I'm Rave. I promise I'm not going to attack you." He glanced at the car and back at her. "They really did a number on your wheels. I'm sorry about that, but you're in Harris Pack territory. It's mating heat time for us and aggression levels are off the charts. May I open the door and check on you? Were you hurt?"

She shook her head.

"No, you're not hurt, or no, I can't come closer? You're safe. My cousin and I are cat-friendly. My older brother's mate, Shannon, is a quarter puma shifter." He grinned. "For real. We're cool with her."

Charma relaxed, willing to believe him, considering she'd fallen in love with a werewolf once. It was possible. "I came to warn you," she managed to get out. "The council accused your pack of attacking one of the prides. They've sent out a joining call."

The handsome guy's smile faded. "They want to talk to us? Is a joining some kind of meeting to ask why we did it? That pride took my brother's mate away from him and they were going to gang rape her to force her to birth a litter of kittens. They weren't exactly willing to just hand her back. We had to kill them to save her. Tell your council *that*."

It didn't shock her that a pride would attack a female part-feline shifter. He'd said this Shannon was of mixed blood, a puma, according to him. It also didn't surprise her that pride males would try to use her body that way. What *did* stun her was that werewolves would kill to retrieve her. He'd said "we", implying a group of them. It was doubtful that a lone wolf could have taken out a pride leader's sons and multiple pride males.

"They wouldn't listen to me or care why you did it. A joining call is when—" Her voice broke and she had to clear her throat. "We have a council that represents all the prides. They ordered all the larger prides to send some of their best fighters to declare war on a common enemy. They plan to attack your pack tomorrow night. At least thirty enforcers will show up."

His eyes widened as he growled softly. She jerked back, scooted on the seat and slid through more broken glass. Pain made her cry out and she jerked her hand up to her chest. The scent of her blood overpowered the odor of her fear and that of werewolf.

"Shit. Why don't you come out? I swear on my life, nobody is going to hurt you. I don't want you to get cut again on the glass. I'm not growling at *you*. I'm just irritated. Why would you warn us? I appreciate it, but I'm curious."

She hesitated before inching toward the door. The guy slowly put his hand inside, popped the lock and swung it open. He backed away to give her room. Charma scooted out to stand. A slight breeze cooled her heated body. She'd broken out in a sweat from her terror.

The guy in the sweater stood about ten feet away with his back to her. He slowly turned around. "Me too," the guy said. "Why would you..."

His voice died when his gaze met hers.

Shock staggered Charma as she stared into the beautiful, sexy eyes that had haunted her for nine endlessly lonely years. Her knees buckled and she knew she would hit the pavement.

Someone stopped her before she impacted. Strong arms lifted her, held her around her waist, but her gaze never left Brand.

Brand couldn't believe his eyes. He blinked a few times but the image didn't change. The tiny woman had striped hair — shades of blonde and brown that fell to her hips. Her big exotic eyes widened. The yellow color within the irises overtook the blue before her body slumped.

Rave grabbed her, tugged her body upward to save her from hitting the street.

Brand lunged forward too. He fisted Rave's jacket with one hand, felt his claws extend, and wrapped his other arm around her too-thin waist. He yanked her against him. A snarl tore from his throat as he realized Charma was actually in his arms.

He feared it was a dream. It was possible he was still at home in bed, suffering mating-heat fever, delirious.

He'd spent the first four years after she'd left searching for her, hoping she'd return to him. It hadn't happened. Part of him had refused to completely let her go but as the years wore on, it had just left him feeling foolish. He'd loved her but she'd chosen to abandon him.

She felt too real in his arms, though, to be a fantasy. He buried his face against her hair, tugging her higher, trying to remember not to crush her frail body. He breathed her in. Her scent was wrong and something about it offended him.

The reason behind it hit as hard as a hammer nailing him in the chest.

He snarled loudly, pain tearing at his heart. He couldn't prevent his fangs from ripping through his gums.

"No!" he snarled. The scent of another male's mark on her nearly drove him insane.

It was faint. Maybe he'd been wrong. He sniffed at her again.

He was just trying to fool his broken heart. The scent was there, she'd really mated someone else. The truth wouldn't be denied. Though weak, the stranger's odor lingered to warn off other males.

It doesn't matter, he decided. *She's mine! I'll hunt the fucker down and tear him limb from limb. I'll rip off his head. No. I'll tear out his heart and feed it to him for taking what's mine. Yeah. That's a good plan.*

"Brand!" His cousin punched his shoulders. "Put her down! Damn it," Rave snarled. "Release. I know you're horny but fuck. Control yourself."

Brand shook off Rave and stumbled, still holding Charma. He nuzzled her neck, hoping to soothe her in case he'd frightened her, something he didn't want to do. Her weight was also wrong. She'd lost a lot of it. He turned to lean heavily against the hood of the car and adjusted his grip on her. He kept his nose buried against her hair in the crook of her neck, taking deep breaths to pull more of her scent into his lungs.

She was real. It wasn't a dream or a fever-induced fantasy. Charma was in his arms, frail and bleeding. The smell of her blood had him battling to keep his skin. The animal inside wanted out to hunt and kill every male whose stench still hung in the air. They'd attacked her car, could have killed her.

He snarled, resisting the urge but only because it meant he'd have to put her down. It wasn't happening. He'd kill them later.

She wiggled her arms against his chest where he'd pinned them but she managed to get them free.

He feared he'd go insane if she fought to get away from him. He prayed she wouldn't do it. He couldn't stand the thought of letting go after he'd finally found her again.

Her thin arms wrapped around his neck instead. She didn't resist, didn't speak, but just clung to him.

"Brand," Rave snarled. "Let her go. I gave my word we wouldn't harm her. She's a little thing and could get hurt if I have to force you to release her."

"Go away," Brand ground out. He really feared he might kill anyone who tried to get between him and Charma, even the cousin he loved as a brother. "Leave us alone."

"I know the heat is bad but damn, you can't go around grabbing stray cats and forcing them to allow you to rub against them. This is embarrassing. I told her she'd be safe."

Brand adjusted her in his arms just to verify that she'd definitely lost weight. His Charma had been curvy and lush. Most she-cats kept a fuller figure than werewolf bitches. He'd loved that about her. She currently could have passed for a lean bitch by the feel of her.

A horrible thought struck. He'd once heard that pride males shunned a mate if she was dying or gravely ill.

"Are you sick, hon?" He was afraid to hear the answer.

"No."

He could breathe again. "You're with me, and this is where you belong. I'm going to take care of you."

She sniffed, wiping her face against him. Wetness seeped through his sweater to his skin, assuring him she'd done it to hide her tears. Her pain, and the possible reason behind it, tore him apart. It didn't matter though. Nothing did, except the fact that she was real. All the bitterness and anger he'd suffered at her loss paled in comparison to having her back in his life. He wouldn't allow her to take off on him again. Once had been bad enough.

"Is he dead?"

She shook her head, clearly knowing what he asked, and pulled back a little. He lifted his gaze to stare into her eyes—the most beautiful he'd ever seen. The love he felt remained strong, tightening his chest. Time had passed but his feelings hadn't changed. She was "the one" and always would be. He knew that deep in his soul, without doubt.

"Brand?" Rave stepped closer. "You know you're acting insane, right? Did you take drugs, trying to ease the heat? Talk to me, man." He glanced at Charma. "Don't be alarmed, she-cat. I'll talk him down. He might be a little out of his head. Please don't claw or bite the crazy wolf. He's harmless."

Brand glared at his cousin. "This is Charma, Rave. My I-fell-in-love-with-a-half-human-spotted-leopard-shifter Charma."

"Shit." Rave gawked, studying her. "She's tiny, man."

"She's five-one. Leopards are small. She used to weigh more." He peered at her, noticing the change in her thin face. "Where are my love handles? You know how much I enjoyed them." His mood darkened, though, when he inhaled that stench coming off her. "I'm going to kill your mate when he comes after you. You're never going to leave me again. I'll chain you to my bed, dig a big-ass moat around my house and fill it with alligators to eat any damn cats who show up. *And* barricade every door and window."

She appeared a little stunned. "Brand—"

"Did you say *mate*? She's mated?" Rave coughed. "I'm sure I heard you say that."

A snarl tore from Brand's throat that he couldn't hold back. Fury gripped him but he tried to regain control. His fangs wouldn't retract for anything but his claws remained sheathed while he stared into Charma's eyes.

"He doesn't matter. You still love me, don't you? I want you to kill me if you say no. That's what you'd be doing anyway."

"I love you, Brand. I always have." Fresh tears filled her eyes. "I never stopped. I had to warn your pack about the joining call. You're in danger."

"I never stopped loving you either." He blinked back his own tears. "You came here and risked your life to save mine, didn't you, hon?"

She nodded. "The prides are going to attack your pack tomorrow night. I couldn't let you die."

Dozens of questions filled his head. How had she known it was his pack that was in danger? Did that mean she'd always known where to find him, yet stayed away? The stabbing sensation to his heart hurt but as he stared into her eyes, it eased. She said she loved him, and she'd left the creep she'd mated to warn him when she thought he was in danger.

She picked me over her mate. That soothed him somewhat.

"Cluster-fuck," Rave growled. "That's what this is."

Brand turned his gaze on his cousin. "It's not that big of a deal. I'll kill the pussy if he comes after her. She's always been mine."

Rave ran his fingers through his hair, gave him a frustrated look and clenched his teeth. "I'm not talking about you and her. We've got to warn the pack and prepare for the arrival of the pride. They obviously don't know this is the absolute worst time for them to attack us. It's going to be a slaughter with all the aggression going on during the heat."

Charma couldn't believe that Brand held her once again. His wonderful scent had changed slightly from what she remembered but it had been nine years. Memories could fade and obviously had. He seemed bigger than she remembered, bulkier, beefier, and stronger. She dangled from his arms, where he kept her face level with his. Her arms were wrapped around his neck and she didn't ever want to let go. She even fought the urge to wrap her legs around his waist, regardless of her skirt, just to press even tighter against him.

"At least thirty pride males will come," she informed them, not sure if she'd mentioned that already after her shock of seeing Brand. "You need to flee the area if that's too many and the mating heat has weakened your pack. They can't really stay for more than a week. Your people can safely return after that time. I've never heard of a joining call lasting longer than that. The males will clash amongst themselves. We don't have a pack mentality. Pride males keep a wide berth of each other unless they're family. They kill each other after extended contact, especially when they aren't in the same pride. There's no sense of hierarchy so they fight for dominance."

Brand stared into her eyes. "The slaughter wouldn't be ours. It will be the pride males. We're really aggressive right now, more so than any other time of the year, and our hold on our humanity is barely there. The only fleeing that will be going on is from the pride that shows up here."

She accepted that. Werewolves were known for fighting more fiercely than pride males. Cats could be flat-out lazy. She knew that from living with one. She relaxed. "You would have been fine if I hadn't come to warn you?"

Rave answered. "No. They could have attacked and taken out many of us if we weren't expecting them. A lone wolf against a large group of cats would assure his death. We're under orders to stay in twos right now but even then, two against thirty would be grim odds."

"A lot of us are ignoring the order too." Brand shot the other male a raised eyebrow. "I don't see you with *your* shadow."

"He stopped to check on the bar. I don't see you with yours, either. Where *is* my youngest brother?" Rave arched an eyebrow.

"Hanging out in my basement. I didn't want to bring him along since I knew something bad had happened. Jeff called." Brand stared at Charma and sighed. "You could have been killed, coming here."

"I knew the risk. I even expected that might happen. I just hoped your pack would allow me to warn them first." She wouldn't lie to him.

He opened his mouth as if to speak but quickly closed it. His harsh features softened as he stared at her. "You're safe, Charma. Nobody is ever going to hurt you."

She believed him.

"I'm never letting you go. Deal with that. You ran out on me once, but don't try to do it again. I want you to swear that you won't leave me. You're mine and always have been. You don't belong to that *pussy*." He snarled the last word. "I looked for you."

That news stunned her. "You did?"

He growled softly. "Did you believe I wouldn't? I was afraid to use your name in case it put you in danger but I put out feelers for a woman with your looks. No one ever reported a sighting."

"I never leave my pride's territory. It's forbidden."

"I hate to interrupt," Rave muttered, "but we need to get her out of the center of town. We've got a lot of strange wolves roaming during mating heat and her being a she-cat… They already attacked her once." He glanced at her car. "And we probably should hide her car before her pride arrives." He met her gaze. "I take it you don't want them to know you warned us?"

"It won't matter. I fled my pride. They'll want me dead regardless of what I do. I knew there would be no turning back and that my life there ended the second I drove away."

Two werewolves in skin approached. Charma's hold on Brand tightened and she stared at them fearfully. Brand growled in response. His hold on her adjusted, one arm releasing her waist as claws slid out of the fingertips of the hand he used to point at the males.

"Stay there. Don't come any closer."

Charma stared at the blond guy who stopped in his tracks, recognizing him, but not the man with him. "Yon?"

His dark gaze fixed on her and he frowned. "How do you know me?"

"The pride council sent your pictures and yours was among them." She glanced at Brand. "That's how I knew this was your pack. They had your picture too. I saw you and knew I had to come."

"Fuck," Rave groaned. "They have pictures of us? Really? I feel totally out of the loop. Should we have pictures of *them*?"

"No. We're more of a threat to them than they are to us," Brand stated. "Guys, this is Charma. If you look at her twice, I'm going to hurt you. You feel me?"

"Shit!" Yon groaned. "Another one? Really? Good thing your aunt was sent away. She'd go nuts if she saw you holding a she-cat that way. I'm guessing you're spending your heat with her?"

"She's mine." Brand's voice deepened into a dangerous tone. "Forever. She's going to be my mate."

Shock tore through Charma. It was one thing to announce it to a male relative, but he was telling pack members he planned to claim her. He turned his head and their gazes met.

"Won't they shun you? Don't get exiled from your pack for me." She kept her voice low. "Please? I couldn't stand it if you're attacked for protecting me."

He emitted a soft rumbling sound but it wasn't scary. He used to do that when she said something that annoyed him but she knew he'd never hurt her. Not Brand. He shook his head and wrapped his arm around her again to hug her tightly.

"They won't kick me out and they sure as hell won't fight me."

She turned her head, still uncertain, but the other men didn't seem aggressive. The blond actually winked.

"She's cute but too thin. She looks like a bitch. I've never seen a she-cat so small, but then I haven't seen many this close up."

"She's lost weight." Brand pushed away from the car. "Do me a favor and hide her vehicle. I'm sure her mate will be searching for her."

"Mate?" The blond gasped and his dark gaze widened. "She's mated already but *you're* going to mate her? Are you nuts? She's taken."

"By me." Brand turned his head to address Rave. "Stash her car, okay? I want to take her home."

Rave nodded. "Go. Keep Braden from the running and I'll call you in a few hours. I'm going to get in touch with my brothers and we'll hold a pack meeting early in the morning to warn everyone of what's coming. I'm worried they'll suspect she warned us when they realize she's gone. They might attack earlier than planned."

"They won't," she informed him softly. "They'll think I ran for other reasons. No one knew about Brand and me. I was too careful, and didn't even take pictures of him with me when I returned to my pride. It would have put him in danger."

"Who's going to attack us?" Yon sounded confused. "What did I miss? It didn't take me *that* long to get here after we heard there was trouble brewing in town."

"Brand, take her home with you and I'll deal with this." Rave hesitated. "Did you run here or drive?"

"Ran."

He held out his keys. "Take the bike. Just leave the keys under the seat. I'll pick it up later. I don't want you walking back with all our visitors in town. They'll scent her. The bike will get you there faster."

"Thanks." Brand slowly lowered her to the pavement beside the bike. He caught the keys Rave tossed to him.

"My keys are still in the ignition of my car," she informed them.

"They could move it anyway." Brand straddled the bike and turned his head. "Get on, Charma."

She didn't allow her skirt to stop her, regardless of how high the material hiked up her thighs. She hugged Brand tightly from behind, not wanting to let him go. He started the bike, and she knew the other werewolves watched them curiously but she avoided their gazes.

Brand lived close to town in a wooded area on a hill. Other houses lined the street but a good distance separated them. He parked the bike next to a red truck but didn't move as the engine died. His hands abruptly covered hers where she hugged his waist.

"We're going to go inside. I'll head downstairs to order my cousin to stay in the basement and then we're going to talk. Swear to me that you aren't going to flee, Charma. Otherwise I'm not allowing you out of my sight. I'd prefer not to take you near Braden right now. He's young and in heat. I don't know if he'll be dressed. Clothes irritate our skin when we suffer this condition. I'd rather spare you that sight, and hell, he could be doing something embarrassing that you really don't want to see."

She peered at the back of his head. He didn't glance at her, just stared straight ahead at his closed garage door. "I'm not going to leave you again, Brand."

His body relaxed and he released her hands. "Good. I'm trusting you to keep your word. You don't know how tough that is for me but I don't really have a choice. Let's go."

The lack of confidence hurt a little but she couldn't blame him. "I swear, Brand. Leaving you was the worst and toughest thing I ever had to do. It tore me apart. But all the reasons I left are gone. This is where I want to be. You have no idea how much I mean that."

He took a deep breath and expelled it slowly. "I'll really tie you to my bed if you make a run for it. Fair warning."

"I understand." She didn't feel threatened.

Brand took Charma's hand, she climbed off the bike, and he slid the keys under the seat. He glanced at her before she followed him up the walkway to his front door. He pushed open the door, which wasn't locked. Lights had been left on and she inhaled. Brand's scent lingered inside his home but she didn't detect any others.

"You live alone?"

"Usually. My cousin is just staying with me during the heat. It's got a full apartment in the basement so he doesn't come up here often. That's why you probably won't smell him."

"My sense of smell isn't as good as yours," she reminded him.

Her gaze left his to study the living room. It had obviously been furnished by a man, his black leather couches, matching easy chairs and bare furnishings testaments to that. She smiled when she spotted the big-screen television that was a prominent feature in the room.

"I know. You probably want to change a lot and you're welcome to do anything to make it more homier." He closed the door, grabbed her and pinned her against the wall. He leaned down until his face hovered inches from hers, his gaze intense. "I'm going to mate you—and I don't care about the bastard who did it before me. I'll bite you until his scent is gone and only mine remains. Deal with that, hon. I'm never going to let you go. I've spent every single day of the last nine years thinking about you. I missed you, and hurt because you weren't with me."

She battled tears and won. "Me too."

"Let me deal with Braden before we talk. Are you hungry?"

"No. I ate a burger on the drive here."

His gaze lowered. "You need to eat more. You're so damn thin. I'm a great cook. I'll feed you until you gain back every pound."

His thoughtfulness was a reminder of what she'd lost and missed. "You'd cook for me? Really?"

His gaze met hers. "I'd do anything for you." His hand shot out and he locked the door. "Make yourself at home. This is yours now too. Ours. I'll be right back."

"Okay."

He spun toward a hallway and disappeared around the corner. Charma remained against the wall where he'd put her and drew in a shaky breath.

Hot tears threatened to spill again. She stood inside Brand's home. She'd dreamed of seeking him out but never thought she'd see the day.

Her gaze roamed the room. She wouldn't change a thing. Her arms hugged her waist as she smiled.

"Home," she whispered.

Chapter Three

Charma sensed Brand behind her and inhaled, his scent flooding her senses. She slowly turned away from the kitchen and found him standing inside the doorway, watching her.

"I was exploring. I love your home."

"Ours," he corrected. "Yours and mine." He took a hesitant step forward. "I keep expecting to wake up and realize this is just a dream." His hand lifted. "Come here, hon."

She went to him without hesitation. Her hand clasped his larger one and he pulled her into a hug. His face burrowed into her hair. He seemed content to just hold her. She rested against him. He'd never left her thoughts, and at night when she'd lain in her bed, she'd relived their months together. It had kept her sane.

She remembered the day Brand had arrived at her apartment in Texas with a blindfold…

~ ~ ~ ~ ~

"You have to wear this, and then just come with me."

She laughed, sure it was some kind of joke. It wasn't. He insisted on covering her eyes after she got into the cab of his truck. Charma had a tough time resisting the urge to reach up and remove the blindfold. "Where are you taking me?"

"We're almost there."

"Is this some kind of romantic picnic? I can smell the trees but there's no exhaust from other cars. We're somewhere out of the city."

"Stop sniffing." He chuckled.

"You know I hate surprises."

"You'll like this one." He paused, and then she had to strain to make out what he said next. "At least I hope so."

"I heard that."

"We're here. Don't move."

The truck stopped and the engine died. She waited impatiently until he got out and opened her door. His fingers curled around her upper arm as she unfastened her seat belt. He led her about ten steps before stopping and positioning himself behind her, one arm wrapped around her waist as he leaned down to press his lips to her ear.

"Have I told you how much I love you?"

Warmth spread through her. "Yes. I love you too. May I look now?"

"Not yet. My roommates are a bunch of idiots and I might have to kill them if I catch them checking out your ass one more time when you stay with me. You're living with the world's biggest grump. It's getting tougher to leave your apartment in the mornings, but it's even worse on the nights we can't spend together. I want to be with you all the time."

Her heart rate increased as his words and their possible meaning sank in. His fingers touched her face and the blindfold came free. She blinked a few times to adjust to the sunshine. The first thing that came into focus was a rustic cabin in the woods. It was a cute single-story A-frame. She forgot to breathe.

"I hope you aren't angry." He dropped the blindfold and wrapped his other arm around her waist to hug her tightly. "I signed a lease. It's ours, Charma."

She latched onto his arms to keep upright when her legs threatened to buckle. She was stunned.

"I know I should have asked you first," he rushed on, "but listen to me before you make up your mind. I can pay the rent, so don't worry about the price. It's not exactly a dream home but it's cozy inside and it's remote enough to give us as much privacy as we want. You might be worried about your car breaking down on the drive out here but I changed a few of my classes to fit with your schedule. I'll drive us to the campus. We won't have to sleep apart anymore or worry about your roommate hearing us have sex."

She recovered from the shock and turned in his arms. The look of anxiety in his expression was clear. "Brand…"

Lines appeared next to his mouth. "I think I thought of everything. I know your pride pays your rent. I talked to your roommate. She swore to say you're still living there if anyone asks. Hell, she was thrilled with the prospect of getting half the rent paid without having to deal with an actual roommate. It was motivation enough for her, and your family won't find out you're living with a werewolf."

Hope was the next emotion that sprang up. "Really?"

Brand grinned. "Yeah."

She turned her head, stared at the cabin. "It's so adorable."

"It's not the biggest place, only one bedroom, but it's in great shape. I had the guys come out with me a few days ago to paint and do minor repairs."

She faced him again but had to blink back tears. "Yes!"

He lifted her off her feet and hugged her tightly. "You haven't even seen the inside."

"I don't care. We'll get to sleep together every night. I hate when we're apart too."

His gaze flicked to her shoulder then back to her eyes. "Sometimes I want to bite you."

That heartfelt confession made her sad. "We can't do that."

"You love me."

"I do, but you're a wolf and I'm a cat."

"You're half cat but I don't give a damn. It doesn't change my feelings or my urges."

"Our families would raise hell if they knew we were a couple. I also told you—"

"Don't." He cut her off. "Don't mention that asshole you're supposed to mate because your leader ordered it. Not now, not today. We're living in the here and now. We have a while before you have to return to your pride."

He was right. She always resisted thinking about when she'd graduate and be expected to return. "Okay."

He slowly eased her back to her feet. "Let's try living together before we have a discussion about that kind of crap."

She could tell he was upset. "I'm so sorry, Brand. I'd want you to bite me if it were possible. I swear I would."

He released her waist and snagged her hand. "I refuse to argue today. Let's go inside. I'll give you the tour."

"Okay." She was willing to let the matter drop.

He fished his keys from his pocket and unlocked the door. Charma tried to take a step inside after he swung the door open but she gasped instead when Brand scooped her off her feet and carried her inside. It was romantic and sweet of him to carry her over the threshold.

The living room and kitchen were one big open space. She was in for another surprise as she studied the new furniture. "You big liar!" She laughed though.

He turned her a bit so she could take in more details of the room. "Sorry about that. I didn't want to buy stuff you'd hate, so that's why I made up the story of needing to replace everything in the living room of the house I rent with the guys. They *do* randomly get sick from drinking but I'd never sink money into that hole. It's like a fraternity, what with five guys living in one house. They destroy everything nice."

She turned her head and stared up at him. "This was so sweet, Brand. It must have cost you a small fortune."

He shrugged. "Not really. I just had to buy stuff for the living room and our bedroom. I got us a king-size bed. No more twin."

She grinned. "I kind of liked having to sleep on top of you so one of us didn't fall out of my bed."

The bedroom was down the only hallway. They passed a bathroom on the way. He paused inside the door. "I just got the bed and a nightstand. There're built-in drawers under the closet. See?"

Charma wiggled until he put her down. The space wasn't big and the bed took up most of it. "A dresser wouldn't fit. I love it just as it is. It's perfect."

"I've already got the most important thing in this room."

She grinned, following his heated stare to the bed. "Yes, you did."

His gaze shifted to her. "I meant you, hon."

She loved him so much it made her chest hurt. "I think we should test out how comfy that mattress is." She reached for the edge of her shirt, tore it up her body and tossed it to the floor.

Brand kicked off his shoes. "Welcome home, Charma. We're going to be so happy here."

"I know we are."

She'd take every precious moment with Brand. She pushed away thoughts of when she'd have to return to her pride. They had a few years before that happened…

~ ~ ~ ~ ~

Brand took a deep breath, pulling her back to the present.

Life had seemed so perfect back then, until it had all come crashing down around her. She'd had to leave the man who'd won her heart and the life she'd loved. The solid arms around her were real again.

"My cousin is safe in the basement. He knows you're here and won't come upstairs if he hears us." He brushed his lips over her forehead. "I want to talk. No. I want to take you to bed and make you mine. I know that's too fast. I know you mated someone else. It pisses me off, smelling him on you. It's faint but it's there. I want it gone."

"I had no choice. I told you that."

He snarled. "We could have found a way. Right now I'm so torn between rage over what you did and relief that you're here."

"You don't understand."

"Nothing could excuse what happened. I came back from my run to discover that you'd taken off."

Charma hated seeing his pain so much that she flinched.

"Don't you dare," he warned. "Don't fear me. You know I'd never hurt you, no matter how angry I am."

"I know that." She wasn't afraid of Brand. "I hate that I did that to you."

He glanced away, took a deep breath, exhaled. His gaze locked with hers. "Me too. I've had a lot of years to think about what I'd do if I ever found you. Bottom line is that you mean more to me than anything else. I'm going to try really damn hard to get past the pain. We were young and we both made mistakes."

"You didn't make any."

"I sure did." Emotion darkened his eyes. "I should have bent you over in front of me and bitten into you to claim you no matter what you said. You were *mine*. It was that simple. I should have listened to my heart instead of hearing your damn excuses. You wouldn't have run out on me if I'd just mated you. It would have been a done deal."

"It would have made things so much worse."

"Nothing could have been as bad as spending year after year obsessing over a woman I had no way of being with."

It ripped at her heart to see and hear such anguish from the man she loved. "I'm so sorry. I don't even know why you still want me after what I did."

"Because you're mine." His chin lifted slightly, showing that stubborn side of him that she remembered so well. "You're the woman I love. Nothing is ever going to change that. We'll work this out. I refuse to do anything less."

His body relaxed and he lifted her suddenly and scooped her into his arms. She stared into his eyes as he carried her through the house toward an area she hadn't explored yet. He strode down a hallway with dark, open doorways, to the lit one at the end. His scent was strong inside the bedroom, assuring her it was his.

She glimpsed a big bed, two nightstands, a chair in a corner and a large television on a dresser, before he took her inside a bathroom. He used his elbow to turn on the light. There were two sinks in a long counter that he eased her butt onto. He released her as he stepped back.

"Give me your hand. Your blood is driving me nuts."

She had forgotten about the cut from the glass. She glanced at it, spotted the red stain on her palm. It wasn't bad. Brand cradled it in his hand and shocked her a little by staring at her while he lifted it to his mouth. His hot tongue cleaned the small wound and his eyes began to shift a little. Dark hair grew out on his cheeks in a soft sprinkling. She lifted her other hand and brushed her fingertips over his jawline and the soft, sparse fur.

"You're having a hard time holding your skin."

He released her hand. "Yeah. I'm really a mess inside right now. Don't worry. You know I'd kill myself before I hurt you."

"I know that." She believed it with her whole heart.

"Good. It would destroy me if I really frightened you. I need to calm down a little and get a handle on things before I mate you. I want it to be good for you but being in heat, I'm barely able to control myself."

"You told me about this." Memories surfaced of him warning her of what would happen when he hit those weeks. They'd joked about who would be hornier while in heat. "We planned to take vacation time from our summer classes and lock ourselves in our cabin so I could take care of you. I just couldn't remember exactly when it happened."

He growled at her. "Now. My wolf is going crazy to mark you." His irises bled black, his wolf showing. The tone of his voice deepened. "Please don't say no. Don't deny me again because, to be completely honest, I'm doing it anyway."

It stunned her that he planned to mate her right off the bat. "It's been a long time since we were together," she reminded him.

"You think I don't know that?"

77

"We've both changed."

He cocked his head, staring down at her. "The feelings are still there. You feel it too."

She refused to deny the truth. "We're both highly emotional right now." His soft growl indicated that he didn't like her words. "I just meant that seeing each other brings back a lot of memories."

"It does," he agreed. "But you're here, and I swore I wouldn't let you go if I ever had you in my arms again. That I'd mate you if it ever happened."

"Don't you want to get to know me again before you make that kind of life-altering decision?"

"No." The determined set of his jaw was something she remembered well.

"We might not click anymore, Brand."

He leaned in, studying her eyes. "We'll adjust to the changes. We were happy once and we'll find that again."

She wished it were that easy. "I hope that's true but a lot has happened over the years. We're strangers now."

"You couldn't have changed that much, hon."

"You don't know that for sure. I know nothing about your life since we parted."

"What do you want to know?"

Her mind blanked. "I'm not sure."

"I missed you. I dreamed about you almost every damn night. Did you miss me? Did I haunt your dreams?"

"Yes."

"Did you wish you were with me?"

"Every day," she confessed.

"Enough said."

It was that simple to him. She envied his certainty. "How can you forgive me? I know you probably felt betrayed. I worried that you'd grown to hate me."

"I tried." He took a step back and blew out a breath. "It just never happened. I just wanted you back. I refuse to let you go a second time. I refuse to spend another nine years missing you and being furious that you're gone. We're mating. That's not up for debate."

Why are you fighting this? He's right here. He wants you and you've always wanted him. Life is never this simple but I want it to be.

She made a decision. They might regret it later but she was willing to risk it.

Charma reached for the bottom of Brand's sweater. "I'm yours now. Take me if you're sure."

His eyes closed and his fangs elongated when his lips parted. It turned her on, seeing his reaction. She shivered with anticipation of what would happen. They'd strip each other, make love, and he'd sink those teeth into the soft part of her shoulder. He'd bite down until he drew blood and she knew it would feel incredible with Brand. It wouldn't hurt or make her scream from the brutality of it. She wouldn't be trapped under a monster intent on staking his claim—one she didn't want.

His eyes snapped open and he inhaled. "What's wrong?"

She pushed away the horrible memories of her first mating. "Nothing."

"I'm scaring you."

"I'm not afraid of you." She hesitated, wondering if she should admit why he'd picked up the scent of fear coming from her.

He studied her eyes closely. "Did he hurt you when he mated you? Is that it?"

The fact that he'd accurately guessed the reason for her hesitancy surprised and saddened her. "You don't want to know."

Rage twisted his features. "I do. I *need* to know. Do you love him?"

"No." Her voice deepened with emotion. "I've always hated him."

He stepped forward, invading her space, and cupped her face in his big hands. "Tell me why you mated him then."

Tears filled her eyes and she had to look away from his. She focused on his lips instead. Ones she'd missed kissing. "It wasn't a love match. I was forced to mate him. I couldn't stand him but he was the pride leader's son. He chose me."

"Then why did you agree to it? For college?" Brand's hold remained gentle but he snarled the words, his anger clear. "I told you I'd pay off the money your pride leader shelled out for your education."

"My parents were in a car accident. It was a rollover crash and the engine caught fire. My father's leg was pinned in the wreckage but he found the strength to protect his mate when my mother's clothes caught fire from flames shooting out of one of the air vents. He tore his leg free and used his hands to put out the flames and smashed through the back window of the car to drag her to safety."

She paused, getting her emotions under control. "Do you know what happens when a pride male is deemed useless? My father's leg was nearly destroyed and he could no longer shift. His healing abilities saved the leg but he couldn't put weight on it. It made him weak in the eyes of the pride. My mother suffered internal injuries and bad burn scars. She's human. They had to take her uterus and she couldn't have more children. There are four of us kids, and I'm the oldest. Three of us are girls." Her gaze lifted to meet his gaze.

"I'm sorry about your parents."

"The pride would have immediately killed my father if I hadn't agreed to the pride leader's terms. If my father died, the only way for my mother to survive would be if another male wanted to mate her or if her children are mated so she's considered part of their families. A new mate's protection would be extended to her children if they were too young to take a mate. Without that protection, she would have been killed and the pride leader would have killed my brother as well. No one would have taken him into their home because he's half human. They couldn't risk sending him to live with humans in case he had the ability to shift. It could have given us away for what we are. My sisters and I would have been handed off to other prides that pay for half-breeds who can't shift. They would have used us as breeders. They—"

"I know what those bastards do. They took my cousin's mate, hoping to force a litter from her."

She nodded. "Breeanna was just nine years old and Megan was thirteen. I was eighteen, and the only one old enough to take a mate to save our family. Adam, my brother, wasn't even a year old at the time." Her gaze held his. She needed for him to see the truth. "The pride leader would have killed my parents and baby brother and sold my sisters into hell if I had run off with you. That's why I had to go back, Brand. My agreement to mate the pride leader's son was all that protected my family."

"Fuck." He closed his eyes and his forehead pressed against hers. "You could have told me. I would have gotten them out."

"And taken them where? Your pack and other prides would have killed them. If you're not inside pride lands, you're inside pack territory, or a lot worse. Either way, they would have been killed and my two sisters turned into breeders. It's sick and wrong, and just the thought of a bunch of males touching my sisters when they hit breeding age…" She took a deep breath. "Do you get that?

82

They don't wait until they're of mating age. Megan would have been sold to those monsters and she hadn't even started high school yet. Hell, she never would have gone, because most prides think educating breeders beyond learning how to read is a waste of money and time. I also was afraid your pack would turn on you if you brought me home. We're natural enemies."

His eyes opened to stare at her. "You and I are not enemies."

"I know that, but does your pack?"

"They'll accept you. Where's your family? I'll bring them here and smooth it out somehow to make sure they're safe. I won't allow anyone to hurt them, Charma. Your sisters won't be touched by anyone."

"They're fine where they are now. Megan mated last year to the younger son of a stronger pride leader in the lands adjoining ours. It was a negotiated deal when they fell in love, between the two prides. Percy, my pride leader, can't harm my family without causing a war he can't win. Their pride is bigger, their family really large, and they'd wipe out every male in my pride if it came down to a fight. Darbin, the other pride leader, accepted our family as his own when Megan mated his son. To harm any members of her family except me would be a grave offense."

"Why not you?" His voice turned into a snarl again, his rage clear.

"Because I'm mated to Percy's son. I'm considered their property and not part of my family any longer. I'm not protected by Darbin."

"You're mine now to protect—and no one will ever hurt you. Why didn't you come to me sooner if you could have left a year ago, after your sister and family were safe?"

"I didn't know where you were. I thought you'd have mated by now anyway, or you wouldn't want me back. I only found you because the prides were declaring war on your pack and I saw your picture."

"Us and our damn rule about not talking about our families." He growled. "I should have given you my address and made you memorize it. I should have ignored you when you made that stupid rule."

"It was safer for us both if we didn't know where our families lived. We knew one day we'd have to part."

"It was stupid. You could have come to me a year ago."

"Why aren't you mated?" It still stunned her.

"Why do you think?" He didn't give her time to answer. "I never forgot you. I dated but they weren't you, Charma. You're the only woman I've ever loved and the only one I ever will. Women find me cold and remote because my heart is taken. None of my relationships lasted. You have owned me since the day you touched my arm and looked up at me, thinking I'd eat you." He smiled. "I wanted to, but not the way you feared." He glanced at her lap. "I wanted to strip you bare and talk you into wrapping those pretty thighs around my face." He met her gaze. "And I still want you to."

He straightened and pulled his sweater over his head. He threw it to the floor and Charma stared at his muscled, tan upper body. He still took her breath away. She studied the changes in the body she'd once memorized, his apparent massive strength. His shoulders had broadened, his biceps were thicker than before, and the inside of his right arm was marred by a new, thin scar. Her gaze lowered to his firm abdomen that rippled with a tight six-pack. More tiny scars adorned his lower stomach. She slid off the counter to reach him, her fingertips tracing a few of them.

"What happened here?"

"Fights. I came home in a bad mood after college. I spent a few years raising some hell. Just don't freak out when you see my back, okay?"

She instantly walked around him and gasped. Two scars ran from his shoulder blades to his mid-back. They were deep ones, white lines on his tan skin. He spun, met her horrified stare and smiled.

"It looks worse than it was."

"I hope you won."

"I did."

"You're bigger." She peered up at him. "Your hair is longer. I love it."

His gaze slid over her body. "You're so thin." His features tensed when he met her gaze. "Give me the address of where you lived. I'll get them and bring them home, Charma. Here with us. I'll take some of my cousins and we'll fight our way in and out. I know it will be tough at first but we'll make it work. I love you, and I'll love them."

She stared at him, confused.

"Your kittens, honey. I'll take them from your pride and we'll raise them." Pain clouded his features. "I swear I'll accept them as if they are my own." He lowered his body to kneel before her. "I know you hear bad shit about wolves killing young that aren't theirs but I swear to you that I'd die to protect them and you. That shit isn't true. They'll be safe here, and loved."

She stepped closer and hugged him, pulling his face against her chest. "I never had kids, Brand. Thank you though." Tears spilled down her cheeks. "That means so much that you'd accept them and get them back for me…if they existed."

He hugged her tightly. "Why are you so thin? I thought maybe having kittens had changed your body."

"You're relieved, though, aren't you?"

He hesitated. "The idea of you carrying another male's offspring hurts but I would have loved them because they were part of you."

All the reasons she'd fallen in love with Brand slammed home. Years had passed, things had changed, but the man she knew still existed. He had a huge heart and the fact that he'd offered to fight to retrieve her children, face danger to do it, just made her more certain she was where she belonged.

"I just wasn't happy. I'm not sick or anything."

"Good." He pulled away to stare at her. "I've missed you so much."

"You have no idea how much I thought about you and how those memories of us together got me through every day."

He released her and rose to his feet. "Let's shower together and go to bed." His gaze raked over her. "No more waiting, Charma. I'm making you mine and that bastard you mated is dead when he shows up here to take you back."

"He won't fight to the death over me. He won't even search unless his father orders him to. He'd do a half-ass job because he won't want me back. He'll be relieved."

"I don't believe that for a minute. Any male would do anything to find you and bring you home."

"It wasn't a love match. We..." She hesitated. "I hated him. It became mutual. I couldn't prevent mating him but I could control certain things. I sneaked pills to avoid ever getting pregnant or going into heat. He never guessed, just thought I was defective as a mate. After a year, he became really angry when I never conceived and he grew bitter." She watched Brand's face, hoping he wouldn't judge her. "Part of the reason he chose me was because he thought I could give him litters of kids and make him a stronger leader when he takes over the pride. I failed to do that and it pissed him off."

Brand didn't appear shocked or horrified by her admission. "I don't blame you. Two people should have kids out of love, not duty."

She relaxed as the tension drained. "I never want any deception between us. I've had to lie for years but I would never do that to you, Brand. I love you too much. I'd never deceive you that way but I had to do it with him."

"He hated you?" Anger deepened his voice. "Why didn't he set you free then? I'm guessing there was no bond formed? He could have just found a new mate without suffering emotionally."

"He wanted to but his father refused to allow it. He wants to stay in his father's good graces by obeying orders, since he has younger brothers who could be chosen to take over the pride leadership instead when Percy steps down."

Anger narrowed his eyes. "I don't like him already. Was he at least good to you?"

She cautiously regarded him. "I don't want you to get angry enough to go after him."

"Son of a bitch," he snarled. "Did he call you names? Was he mean? I know some shifters look down on half-breeds." His hands fisted at his sides. "Did he ever hurt you?"

She hesitated. "You're going to want me naked in that shower...that means you'll see this." She snagged her shirt and carefully removed it. It dropped to the floor and she lifted her arm.

Rage had him sprouting hair, his eyes darkened and his claws shot out of his fingertips. Charma held still, knowing it wasn't directed at her. She still trembled. He moved slowly, though, his hand gentle as he avoided touching her with the sharp points of his nails. He held her upper arm and turned it slightly to examine the dark bruises—marks from fingers encircling her arm just above where he touched. He snarled and his gaze lifted.

"He did this to you?" His voice came out sounding gravelly, deep and harsh.

"Yes. It happened last night. We live in separate parts of the house and rarely see each other. He sought me out in my room. I didn't want him touching me so I fought. I got away but he was pretty angry." She tugged out of his hold and reached up to grip her hair, pulling the long curtain of it away. She slowly turned, grateful that she couldn't see his face when she presented him with her back. "This is the last of it."

The howl made her jump, the sound deafening inside the small bathroom, and every instinct urged her to flee. The smell of his rage nearly suffocated her as it filled the room but Charma held still, waiting for him to calm. She lowered her head in sadness.

"I'm going to kill him," Brand swore.

He breathed hard, nearly panted, and Charma turned her head enough to catch a glimpse of her reflection in the mirror. Four bruises marred her back from where she'd been punched as she'd struggled to get away from Garrett. They actually appeared to be a lot better than they had when she'd dressed earlier that morning before she'd left the house. Her shifter genes allowed her to heal quicker than a normal human.

"Did he force you? Did that son of a bitch *rape* you? Did he allow other men to touch you? I want their names if that happened. I'll track down all of them! I'll kill each one! I'll—!"

"Calm down," she ordered.

She faced him. Any other werewolf looking that feral would have sent her bolting for her life. He'd totally lost his face—his nose pressed forward, lengthened, along with his jawbone, and his fangs elongated. His eyes had shifted too, narrowed. Wolf eyes watched her.

Black hair covered his lower face and hid most of his sexy chest and arms. She took a step closer to him and brushed his soft pelt of fur with trembling hands. She pressed her face against him.

"No one else touched me, not even him. He hasn't for years; I was smart enough to avoid him. He found other females to occupy his time when he believed I wasn't able to conceive. I'm okay, Brand. I promise you that, and he's not worth it. Just hold me, okay?"

His arms wrapped around her and she stood there inside his embrace for a long time, until warm skin returned and his breathing slowed. He kissed the top of her head before easing away. She wondered if he'd still want her, knowing she was emotionally damaged. Tenderness was reflected in his gaze when she braved looking up at him.

"You never need to fear anyone again and I would never abuse you."

"I know."

"I'd rather die," he whispered.

"I know that too."

"Okay. I'm still going to kill that son of a bitch, but that's another day."

She didn't protest. A part of her had always known if Brand ever found out about what Garrett had done to her, even if he'd moved on and mated another woman, he'd have paid her mate a visit to make the abuse stop. It was just the kind of wonderful person he was. When they'd watched the news, he'd always grumbled that someone should take out violent jerks who picked on the weak.

"I need to calm down a bit." He took a deep breath. "Shower here and I'll use the bathroom down the hall. We'll meet in my room in about fifteen minutes." He fled before she could protest and closed the door behind him.

Charma watched him disappear and worry struck. Would he change his mind about wanting her? She wasn't the same woman he'd once loved. She'd been mistreated by a mate and maybe he feared she'd take that out on him. Or worse, maybe he'd lost all respect for her because she'd allowed her life to become such a nightmare despite doing it for her family's safety.

She turned with a heavy heart, staring at Brand's shower. She knew he wanted her to wash off as much of the scents from her old life as possible. Using his shampoo, conditioner and soap wouldn't completely rid her of Garrett's mark but it would make her smell more familiar to Brand, more like his.

Chapter Four

Brand stormed down the hallway and managed not to punch his fists through the walls. He saw red from the rage that pulsed through his entire body as if it were a living thing. He paused by the guest bath, took a deep breath and stepped inside to flip on the light. He managed not to slam the door behind him. He met his reflection in the mirror and winced at some of the hair he hadn't been able to control when he'd returned to skin.

Charma had been abused, hit. She was sickly thin. Her clothes had hidden the sight of her rib. She appeared half starved.

He closed his eyes, careful not to pierce his bottom lip with his fangs when he bit down to muffle another howl of rage. The urge to shred the male who'd forced her mating nearly drove him into hunt mode.

It had been difficult, picturing his Charma out in the world living without him. He'd imagined her many times—mated, with kids. It had tortured his soul. It had bothered him, thinking she might be happier with someone else, but he'd never considered that she'd been forced into a hellish nightmare of shifter politics. She'd been traded by her parents to the pride leader's son. He understood their motives but it enraged him. He'd rather die than hand any child, even a grown one, over to someone to abuse.

Do her parents know how she was treated?

93

He shoved that thought back. He'd kill them himself if they had stood back and allowed it to happen. His rage continued to build. *They had to realize something was wrong. She's lost so much damn weight.* He forced his breathing to slow when he became agitated enough to pant.

I can't mate her right now.

That thought made his wolf recoil in protest. She was too thin, too weakened, and probably too scared to have a male go at her the way he would if she were naked on his bed. He might accidentally hurt or frighten her. Neither was an option he was willing to risk.

Most, if not all, of his resentment toward Charma for leaving him faded. She'd loved him but she'd also loved her family. He understood how far someone would go to protect blood. He hadn't been blessed with siblings but his cousins might as well be his brothers. There wasn't much he wouldn't do for them. Charma had been put in a hellish situation and made a deal with the devil to keep her family safe.

They gave my Charma to that prick.

He wished she'd told him everything in the past. He would have moved heaven and hell to bring her entire family into Harris territory. He'd have probably upset her by tearing into her parents a bit over their eagerness to sacrifice her future for their own, but younger siblings were involved. He hated to admit it but he could see why they'd do it. It wasn't something he agreed with but if she'd just been honest, he could have prevented them from making the choice they had.

His uncle would have agreed to accept Charma's family into the pack but his aunt would have gone on a rampage. He winced, remembering what she'd done to Anton's mate. Aunt Eve was the entire reason a bunch of feline shifters were about to attack the pack. She'd put her own son's mate in danger because she'd been desperate to be rid of a she-cat.

He and his cousins had rescued Shannon from the fate Eve had tried to deal her. There was no telling what underhanded thing his aunt would have attempted to do to Charma and her family if he'd moved them into the territory. It no longer mattered though. Eve wasn't a problem since she'd been banished from the pack, but in the past, she could have posed a deadly threat.

Either way, they couldn't change history. Charma was in his bathroom showering. He wanted to claim her but it wasn't going to be easy or fast. The son of a bitch she'd been forced to submit to had done damage. She needed time to heal and get to know him again in order to feel totally safe in taking a new mate. His wolf didn't agree, too eager to claim her. It was hard to control the urge since the animal was too close to the surface to be pushed back.

"Goddamn heat," he ground out.

He'd never be able to keep totally in control of his body if she were naked in his arms. He was man enough to know his limitations and loved her enough to admit he posed a real danger to her in his condition. Males in heat weren't known for their gentleness or their ability to contain the lust that overcame them during sex. She could take him in the past but he wasn't so certain about now.

He smiled at the memories of Charma from their time together. She'd been a tough little thing, aggressive as hell in heat, and she could give as good as she got. He'd never worried about crushing her or accidentally snapping something. She'd had generous curves, meat on those bones, and the plushest ass he'd ever had the pleasure of pounding against when he'd taken her.

His dick chose that moment to painfully throb as if it had a heartbeat. If it weren't for the thick jeans, it would be pointing straight out. His balls began to ache and he groaned.

"Goddamn it," he hissed between still-clenched teeth. "I'm going to die." He gazed at his reflection. "I'm never going to survive having her under my roof, smelling her and wanting her."

He kicked off his shoes, denting a cabinet in his haste to get the things off, and jerked open the front of his pants. He hadn't bothered with underwear and his cock sprang free. It barely eased the pain as he shoved the material down his legs. He nearly tore off the glass shower door to get inside the stall. He turned on the cold water and it blasted his body, shocking chill taking his breath. He stood there, endured it, but it didn't do a thing to his lower half.

"Fuck."

He reached for the body wash, dumped a handful into his palm and leaned back against the wall. He fisted his shaft, turned his hips enough to avoid the water and squeezed his fingers around his swollen cock. His eyes closed as Charma's image filled his head. He frantically moved his hand from the base of his dick to the head, applying enough pressure and pace to feel really good. He imagined he was inside her again.

He braced his legs, threw back his head and sealed his lips. He'd never forget how damn tight Charma had been, how wet and hot. Her muscles squeezed him better than his fist ever could. Then there were the sounds she always made when he fucked her hard and fast.

His Charma had always purred for him, urged him on, her legs wrapped tightly around his hips. She had a habit of raking her nails down his spine until she could grab his ass and pull his hips even tighter against her soft thighs. He'd feel her climax. She always screamed out his name, her pussy tightening around him as she trembled from her release…

He groaned as he came. Streams of semen shot from the tip of his cock as pleasure gripped him. His hips bucked from the intensity and the pain disappeared.

He panted, opened his eyes and stared at the tile wall opposite him that he'd just decorated. His hand eased off his cock—it had barely softened—and he turned into the water to wash off the soap. He dunked his head, shook it, and reached for the body wash again.

Great. That will last me for a little while before it starts again. He scrubbed his body to wash away the dried sweat from fighting and reached up to grasp the removable showerhead. He rinsed away all traces of evidence that he'd jacked off inside the stall as he washed down the tile. He replaced the showerhead, turned off the water and pushed open the glass door.

"I'm going to be in here every half hour, repeating this." Disgust welled at his lack of control. He dried off, avoiding his cock, which still strained from the constant state of arousal he knew wouldn't leave him until mating heat ended. All he could do was pray he'd find the strength to grab for soap instead of Charma.

He realized he hadn't remembered to bring a change of clothes. He wrapped the towel around his waist and quickly exited the bathroom. If he hurried, it would only take him a minute to slip down the hall, enter his room and get dressed before she finished her shower. The woman used to spend an eternity showering. He hoped that hadn't changed.

The bedroom was empty when he stepped inside but he didn't hear water running in the other room. He darted to his dresser, opened the lower drawer and chose a pair of sweatpants. The bathroom door opened behind him and he jerked upright, turning.

Charma had washed her hair. Pink skin shone from the warm water and she was wrapped in his favorite blue towel. The tops of her shoulders and her thighs were revealed. He knew she didn't have anything on under it and his cock stiffened in response.

He wanted her so bad it was difficult to remain still. He struggled with his choices—lunge at her or flee the room. She was just too tempting, too sexy. Images of all the things he wanted to do to her filled his mind and kept him from returning to the bathroom down the hall.

She smiled and her gaze lowered to his towel. He couldn't move, his legs seemingly rooted to the carpet. More blood flowed into the part of him that she stared at.

Yeah, she's looking at you. She can't miss seeing you when you're pointing right at her and lifting the damn towel. He reached down, pushed his cock against his thigh and kept his palm over it. *Ouch. I know you don't want to bend but we don't want to scare her either.*

"You're definitely bigger."

"Oh hell. Pretend you don't notice."

Her gaze lifted as she stepped closer to him and his bed. "Why would I do that? Drop the towel. Let me see how much you've grown."

Panic seized Brand. "Don't come near me." She froze and he wanted to kick his own ass when he saw uncertainty on her features. "I'm sorry," he got out. "You just need to stay back."

"Why?" Pain flashed in her beautiful eyes. "Don't you want me, Brand? Did you change your mind about mating me?"

"No. I mean, I do. You have no idea how bad I want you...and to claim you as my mate." He growled.

"Then why can't I approach you?"

Honesty is best. Yeah. "I'm afraid I'll hurt you. My control is shaky and I think we should wait until I'm out of heat to do this. That will give you some time to put on some weight and heal up. It will also guarantee that I'll be as gentle as possible when we seal the bond without causing you any injuries."

She stared at him, seemingly stunned.

"I'm dangerous," he whispered. "To you. Right now. I wouldn't mean to be but I'd be too rough. I want you too much. My dick is in charge, and yeah, I want you. I would never forgive myself if I caused you pain but I know I will."

"I don't believe that." She glanced down his body. "You're bigger and stronger but that doesn't scare me."

"Charma?" He waited until she met his gaze. "Trust me. You've never seen me in heat."

"It can't be worse than *my* heat when I was with you."

"It is." He swallowed hard, his cock throbbing against his palm through the wet towel. "I'm more aggressive than you ever were at your worst. I need to go into the bathroom right now and you need to stay there. I'll handle my own needs. I thought I would have more time in between but that was before I saw you in so little, looking so damn sexy. I have to handle this. Me. Shit!"

He bolted around her and into the bathroom she'd just vacated, slamming the door between them.

He locked the door. The Charma he knew would follow him. She'd always hated it when he walked away from a disagreement.

The last time he'd done it flashed through his head and he spun, his hand bracing on the solid wood. *What if she takes off again? What if I go out there and she's fled?*

He nearly unlocked the door but fear kept him from doing that. He spun, his actions jerky as he yanked open the shower door and turned on the water. He'd be fast.

She wouldn't leave. I'd rather her think I'm a jerk than screw this up by hurting her.

Charma couldn't help but feel hurt. She turned around and heard the water come on. *He's going to handle his own needs?* She stared at the door as anger hit.

She tried to twist the door handle but found it locked, preventing her from following him. "Damn it." Her other palm slapped the wood barrier. "Brand?" She called out his name. "Open the door."

"Go eat something," he called out. "Or rest. I'll be out soon."

"Damn it, Brand. Let me in there. I'm not fragile!"

He didn't answer. She turned her head and pressed her ear against the wood, listening. Her keen hearing picked up faint noises over the water. She bit her lip when she heard his breathing increase and a slight slapping sound, guessing what he was doing in there to "handle his own needs".

More like fisting his own cock. She didn't move away until she heard him come.

Her body responded to his throaty groan, one she remembered too well. Brand had no idea how wrong he was if he thought she'd make it easy for him to keep her at arm's length. It had been a while since she'd suffered the effects of heat but it wasn't something anyone forgot. He needed her and she wanted him. It was incredibly sweet that he was so concerned with her safety but it was also frustrating.

She knew she faced no danger from him, regardless of how horny or aggressive he got during the worst of the heat. He refused to listen to her though.

A plan formed and it made her smile.

She'd actually make it impossible for him to resist nature's call.

One quick tug and the towel dropped at her feet. She turned to face the bed. *I just need to get him on it with me.* She glanced at the door, heard the water shut off and moved, climbing onto his mattress before he came out.

Charma centered her body on his bedspread and stretched out on her back. She moved her hair out of the way by shoving it into a damp pile above her head. Her feet pressed against the bed to angle her hips just enough to ensure what he'd see when he opened that door. She spread her knees wide.

Her gaze remained on the bathroom door as she inserted a finger into her mouth, wet the tip and let her palm trail down her body. It slid between her breasts, over her stomach to her pussy. She needed to be turned on. He'd always gone insane when he'd picked up her scent when she was in need of sex.

A mischievous grin curved her lips as she thought back to the past to help her get in the mood.

She pressed her fingertip against her clit and rubbed small circles. Just thinking about Brand made her nipples hard. She held her breath to suppress the sound of pleasure as her finger ignited her body, making it warm and tingly.

Memories of the first time she'd gone to bed with Brand drifted through her thoughts. They'd dated for over a month before she'd known the time was right. She'd fallen in love with him and figured he felt the same, since he never pressured her for sex. She'd been terrified her she-cat instincts would react to him being a werewolf…

~ ~ ~ ~ ~

"Let's go camping."

He gaped at her. "What?"

"You know the woods where we run when you shift? Why don't we take a tent and sleep out there for a night?"

103

He frowned.

"Don't tell me you're grown too soft."

The insulted expression on his face had been amusing. "Of course not. I love roughing it."

The muscles of her lower belly clenched as an image of Brand tearing her out of her clothes flashed. She bet he would do that. "So let's camp tonight. We don't have classes tomorrow. It's midweek so nobody should be out there."

Brand braced his hands on his hips and studied her a bit too closely. "It's a bad idea."

"Why? Do you think it will be too cold?"

He sighed and let his hands drop to his sides. "I wouldn't trust myself all night with you."

She grinned. "Good. You bring the tent and blankets. I'll bring the food. We'll probably need a lantern too. My night vision isn't as good as yours and I want to see everything in that tent."

He moved fast, gripping her hips. "What does that mean?"

She took a deep breath for courage. "I've never done this before but I want you. I know you want *me*. I think it's safer for both of us if we don't go to your place or mine, where we could be overheard. You get growly when we kiss and I start purring. They'll think we're into weird fetishes if we're loud."

Brand's complexion paled. "You're a virgin?"

"No. I told you I had a boyfriend for a short time. I meant I've never had to be the one to make the first move. I'm talking about sex. As in, I want to have it with you."

"Thank god."

"Are you happy that I'm suggesting we finally go to bed together or that I'm not a virgin?"

"Both." Brand grinned. "I've been killing myself being patient because I know I scare you a bit but the idea of being your first terrified me."

"Why?"

"It's always painful for women and I don't ever want to hurt you, hon."

She knew at that moment that she'd made the right choice. "Camping tonight then."

"Yes."

"And bring a lantern." She raked her gaze over his chest. "I don't want to miss a thing. I've tried to imagine you naked but I have a feeling the real thing is going to be better."

"I think that's *my* line."

They gathered everything they needed for their getaway and set off for a romantic tryst in the woods.

Brand took things leisurely enough to drive her crazy as he stripped her bare and explored every inch he exposed. It turned her on, the way he growled as he brushed kisses over her lower stomach and spread her thighs to get access to her pussy.

"I plan to eat you alive."

She didn't laugh, was too turned on to do more than pant. "I hurt for you," she admitted.

Brand had an amazing mouth, and the things he could do with it made her grateful they were miles away from civilization. She cried out loudly when he made her come twice before easing up her body and penetrating her. The sensation of him filling her was something she'd never forget. Brand took his time to help her adjust to his size. He used slow, shallow thrusts to fit his thick cock snugly inside her body. He stared into her eyes when he was all the way inside and told her how beautiful she was to him.

"Move," she pleaded.

"I don't ever want to forget this moment," he whispered.

"We won't," she swore, wrapping her legs higher around his waist and wiggling. "Kiss me."

"I'd do anything for you."

He kissed her then until she was wild beneath him, bucking her hips and clawing his back. It was nearly torture, having him inside her but not moving. She wanted him to thrust in the worst way.

"Please," she rasped.

He shifted over her, using his arms to brace his weight and cage her under him at the same time. "You're so damn tight. Am I hurting you?"

"Only if you don't move."

"There's no going back, Charma. You're mine now."

In a sudden frenzy, he took her. Only she and Brand existed. Passionate kisses and his body taught her the meaning of being loved until she climaxed a third time. She didn't even care when he tore his mouth away from hers to grip her neck with his teeth. No fear surfaced as those sharp fangs raked her tender skin. He didn't bite down but instead muffled a loud groan as he came seconds later.

He made love to her all night. As dawn broke, he pulled her close and she knew she belonged in his arms forever…

~ ~ ~ ~ ~

Charma pushed away the memories when tears filled her eyes. She'd stopped touching herself and some of her passion had cooled. She'd been young back then, and foolish. She'd hoped Garrett would change his mind about forcing her to be his mate. "Out of sight, out of mind" had been the motto she prayed he'd take to heart. She had everything to lose otherwise.

Brand.

"Pull it together," she whispered, blinking rapidly and taking a few deep breaths. *He's in the next room. You didn't lose him forever.*

Just for nine years. She focused on the future and played with her clit. Brand was going to come out of the bathroom and she wanted to be ready for him to take her. She was with him again. Nothing stood in their way now.

Chapter Five

Brand knew he had to leave the bathroom. No doubt Charma had guessed he'd been jacking off. He should have left the bedroom and gone to the one down the hall but he'd been too horny, too close to lunging at her, and hell, it was done. He still needed pants. He wrapped a fresh towel around his waist, certain he could spend a few minutes with her to smooth things over before he made a fool of himself again by needing to take care of business.

He opened the bathroom door and the scent hit him like a sledgehammer as his gaze locked on Charma. He dropped to his knees before he even realized his legs had collapsed under him.

She was naked on his bed, thighs spread, her finger on her clit, taunting him. She met his gaze, even paused the slow stroking that aroused her, filling the room with her sweet scent.

Her other hand rose and she hooked a finger at him. "Come here, baby."

She's going to kill me. No need for mating heat to do it. His gaze focused on her pussy—pink and spread apart enough for him to see the glistening proof that she wanted him. He growled, the sound bursting forth as his fangs pierced his gums. She didn't flinch or show fear though. She smiled instead when he jerked his attention to her face.

"Come get me, Brand. I'm all yours."

Her voice came out husky with a catch to it, telling him she was close to coming. He dropped forward to his hands and crawled toward her. Fearing for her safety, he tried to stop but nothing was going to draw his wolf away from her. It was in control.

"That's it." She bent her arm beneath her head and watched him as she pressed her heels against the mattress. He almost went insane when she tilted her pussy for him to view it better. "See something you want? It's yours."

"Charma," he snarled. His hand flattened on the bed when he reached it. "I'm dangerous."

"I love it when your eyes bleed black and you get all gruff and growly. I want you so much. Can you see? Want to taste?" She moved her heels apart, spreading her legs farther and pulling her finger away from her clit. "Do you want me? Take me, Brand."

He snarled again, fighting hard to hold back his wolf, who wanted to lunge at her. His claws dug into the mattress as they elongated, his inner beast winning. His cock stiffened further and he panted as sweat broke out over his entire body. She had no idea what she did to him.

"Want my thighs around your head? Or do you want me to roll over so you can mount me from behind?" Her body tensed and he feared she'd do that.

He moved fast to keep her thighs apart and held her down, careful of his claws. His gaze lowered to her swollen clit and the pinkest, prettiest pussy he'd ever known.

The battle was lost. He salivated as he breathed her in, snarled, and his tongue came out. One swipe over her pussy and her addictive flavor shattered any resistance he had left.

Charma knew she should be afraid since she'd just tempted a wild beast into coming at her, but it wasn't fear she felt as Brand's tongue drove inside her pussy. Pleasure was instant. He snarled again, a vicious, scary sound, but she didn't care. He nuzzled in tightly until his nose rubbed against her swollen clit. She nearly came just from him touching her and having his tongue inside her. It was thick, stretching her tense vaginal walls. He seemed to want to get as deep as he could reach.

Her legs adjusted, her feet found purchase on the sides of his back, allowing her to draw her legs up enough to give him as much access to her pussy as he wanted. His hands on her thighs, holding her open, were bruising but she'd heal. It didn't hurt.

Another snarl tore from him, his chest rumbled under her feet and he pressed tighter, shaking his head a little. She moaned. His tongue withdrew slightly before pushing deeper and he added an up-and-down, nodding motion.

She reached for him with both hands and her fingers slid into his hair, holding him tightly to her. His nose rubbed her clit as he began to fuck her with his tongue. Pleasure made her pant, purr and ache. Her nipples throbbed, her belly quivered, and she screamed out his name. The climax tore through her. Brand snarled again, growing wilder as he got the first taste of her release.

He'd never been this aggressive in the past—close, but not as rough. She didn't mind, and she had no complaints when he tore his face away, forcing her to release his hair. She held his black gaze when he stared at her.

"Damn it, Charma." He didn't sound human. "Forgive me."

"It's okay, baby."

He rose, grabbed her and rolled her over before she knew what he had in mind. A hand dug under her belly and lifted until she ended up on her knees. Her hands shot out to brace her body as two hundred-plus pounds of out-of-control male curved over her from behind.

He froze but she didn't. His hot, thick cock pressed against her inner thigh. She wiggled her ass against him.

"Fuck me," she moaned. "Make me yours."

His arm hooked more firmly around her waist and he adjusted his legs to the outside of hers to align their hips. To help him, Charma arched her back, pushed her ass higher and spread her thighs a little wider apart. He didn't even need to use his hands to guide his cock to her. It seemed to know where it wanted to be as the thick crown pressed against the entrance of her pussy and he drove home.

She cried out as he stretched her. There had been no time to adjust but it hurt so good. Ecstasy shot straight to her brain before he nearly withdrew from her body. Her muscles clamped down, trying to keep him from totally leaving her, but she didn't need to worry about that.

Brand's arm tightened on her waist to make sure she couldn't get away. Not that she wanted to. His other hand slammed down on the bed next to hers. His claws tore through the bedspread and into the mattress as he braced his weight. His hips slammed against her ass, burying his cock deeper inside her.

"Yes," she moaned.

He growled, his face buried in the curve of her shoulder as he curled more closely around her and pounded his cock into her pussy in fast, long strokes that gave her ultimate pleasure. His shaft seemed to swell as he fucked her frantically, the friction sweet and intense at the same time. Her eyes closed. She couldn't think, could just feel, and another climax built until she screamed his name.

He slowed his movements a bit and withdrew the arm from around her waist. She had to brace to keep from collapsing onto her stomach but she heard his quick intake of breath and turned her head. He had bitten into his wrist—and it was suddenly in front of her.

She knew what he expected of her, and she was happy to do it. It took effort to keep her balance while grabbing hold of his arm and pulling it to her mouth.

The craving to taste his blood wasn't a shifter trait she'd inherited but it would help seal the bond, a form of acceptance.

He fucked her faster as she sucked on his wrist. It seemed to excite him more. Brand howled as he started to come so hard she could feel his semen marking her body. His hips bucked as he drove into her deeply and stayed there, grinding against her ass in sharp jerks with every hot blast of his release that filled her. He snarled as he dropped his head. She tilted hers to the side to bare her shoulder, to give him what she knew he wanted.

His fangs scraped the soft part of her shoulder. His tongue darted out to wet the area before he bit down. Sharp teeth pierced her skin and the pleasure and pain blurred as she came again, her vaginal muscles clamping around his cock. He bit her harder, until his jaw locked while he marked her with his bite and saliva. She released his wrist and he hugged her around her waist again.

Time blurred and she was grateful he held her so securely, sure she'd collapse under him if it weren't for his arm supporting her. He adjusted his body a little, pulled them up slowly, but refused to unlock his jaw, which still imprisoned her shoulder. He kept their bodies connected with his cock buried inside her pussy as he lifted her onto his lap and sat up straight. He hugged her against his chest. She leaned back to press firmly against the solid wall of his body.

The feel of his teeth embedded in her flesh started to ache as the sex haze faded but she didn't complain. She knew why he did it. He wanted to mark her well, make her take as much of him as possible as his saliva was introduced into her bloodstream, to be certain their mating took hold. She rubbed his shoulders, caressed him, to silently convey that she was okay. She couldn't speak, still too out of breath from what they'd done to form words.

He finally withdrew his fangs and licked at the blood that welled up from his bite marks. His hot tongue soothed away the pain. He nuzzled her head.

"I love you, Charma," he rasped against her skin. "You're mine, hon. Forever."

"Forever," she agreed.

Brand breathed deeply. She knew he breathed in her scent and she smelled like him now, was totally his. There would be no lingering traces of the male who'd once claimed her.

"I didn't hurt you?"

She smiled. "That was amazing."

He hugged her closer and she felt his cock stiffen inside her, grow thicker, and she wiggled her ass on his lap. He groaned and his arms adjusted until he cupped her breasts in both his big palms.

He slid her taut nipples between his fingers and thumbs, gave them a pinch, and she moaned.

"Tell me no," he groaned, his head turning as his lips brushed kisses over the sensitive skin of her neck. "Otherwise I'm going to fuck you for hours. Years. Decades. God, I missed you."

She lifted off his cock and he growled in protest but released her. She turned on her knees to stare at him and saw the hungry look he gave her. She'd missed him too. He looked so incredibly sexy and so hers. She didn't hesitate to climb on his lap, facing him, and use his broad shoulder to brace herself with one hand while her other lowered to grip his cock.

He groaned and closed his eyes.

"You *are* bigger," she leaned forward to lick the skin beside his nipple. Her teeth nipped him. His cock jerked in response and seemed to harden even more in her hand. "Sexier. So hot, baby."

She aligned the crown of his shaft under her and sank down. She purred as his cock filled her, adjusting her legs to wrap around his hips and gripping his shoulders with both hands. She used her hold on him to lift up and drop down on his cock. Brand snarled in response and his hands cupped her ass. He squeezed both cheeks and pulled her against his hips.

His head lowered, black eyes opened, and he rose to his knees. Brand moved them, Charma wrapped around him, until the padded headboard bumped her back.

"Ride me. God, I love it when you do."

She smiled as he released her ass and clung to the top of the headboard to brace his body. Her arms wrapped around his neck, and she used her thighs, locked around his hips, to slowly slide up his chest, her butt moving up and down, riding his cock. She purred louder while kissing his throat, jaw, and finally his mouth.

She avoided his fangs as their tongues met. He growled when his knees shifted a little under them and his hips bucked up, driving his cock into her deeper. She tore her mouth from his to avoid biting. She did that to his throat instead, her teeth closing on the spot she remembered he most loved to be nipped.

Hair broke out over his skin where her hands touched and she knew he was losing control. She didn't care. He'd never totally shift on her. She never minded when he lost some of his skin, appreciated being able to turn him on that much, and she'd half expected it when he'd slammed her back against the padded headboard. His hands released the top of it to grab her ass instead. He wildly fucked her, rough and deep.

The headboard slammed against the wall, their breathing turned harsh and she bit him harder, drawing a little blood, even with her flat teeth, further sealing the bond. She wished she were in heat. Some fangs and claws would really send him over the edge. The climax tore through her and Brand growled loudly as he came too. Her muscles twitched strongly around his driving cock.

117

They stilled, panting, and Charma licked at the wound she'd inflicted, marking him as her own. This time she wouldn't feel guilt if she scarred him. He was her mate, and he'd never have to explain to another female about who had put scars on him.

"Mine," she whispered against his skin.

"Fuck yes," Brand rasped. "I'm all yours."

The door to the bedroom exploded open and Brand snarled. His head whipped around to face the intruder. His entire body tensed, preparing to attack to protect his mate.

He glared at his cousin who stood in the open doorway. Braden wore jeans, nothing else, and was out of breath.

"What do you want?" Brand made sure Charma's body was hidden by his own.

Braden's eyes widened as he gawked at them. His gaze darted to Charma and he swallowed hard. "I thought you were under attack. I heard furniture breaking and you yelled."

Charma cleared her throat. "I take it this is your cousin? Don't move unless you make him turn around first, and hand me something to wear, please."

Brand muttered a curse. "Turn around, damn it. Stop gawking at my mate."

The guy actually blushed and spun on his heel. "I'm sorry. I thought someone broke in. I was coming to save you. Shit."

Brand resented withdrawing from Charma's body and having to release her. He grabbed a pillow, held it up, and she clutched it against her body. He got off the bed, shot another glare at his cousin's back, and picked up the sweats from the floor where he'd dropped them earlier to yank them up his legs.

He tore open drawers, removed a T-shirt and threw it at the bed. A pair of drawstring shorts followed. Then he walked to his cousin, slapped a hand over the curve of his shoulder and pushed him forward into the hallway. He would have closed the door but it was broken from Braden's entry. He settled for pulling it near the busted frame to give Charma some privacy.

"What did I say about not coming up here?"

Braden sighed, turned his head and met his gaze. "I'm sorry, man. I really thought you were in trouble. It sounded like all hell was breaking loose."

Brand released him. "I appreciate the concern but as you could see, the only one in danger is you."

"Me?" Confusion clouded Braden's features before he stumbled back a few steps. "Hey, that's not funny. I thought I was coming to the rescue."

"Tell you what, don't do it again unless I yell your name."

"Your neck is bleeding."

Brand grinned. "I know."

"Freak." Braden backed up more. "You let her bite you? Really?" He stared at the marks. "She's got smooth teeth? I thought she was half shifter."

"She's my mate." He touched the tender spots. "Wait until she's in heat." His grin spread. "It's the only time she grows fangs."

"She doesn't totally shift?"

"Nope."

"I guess that's good. I mean, that would be too weird if you tried to fuck out of skin. I don't even think that would be possible. It would be —"

"Shut up. You're rambling."

"Sorry." Braden sniffed. "Lucky bastard," he whispered. "I need to go to the running. I need a woman."

"No, you're not going."

"My hand is tired and you only gave me three porn videos. I've watched them a dozen times."

"Switch up. Remember what I told you. It'll help you keep your muscle tone balanced in both your arms."

"That's not funny, damn it. You're getting some. Why can't I? I'm —"

"Not going out," Brand ordered him. "Rave specifically told me to keep you in. Charma said the prides have called a joining."

"What the hell is that? It sounds kinky."

"It's where the prides get together to pool their resources and they plan to attack us tomorrow night."

"No shit? Why would they do that? It's stupid."

"They're angry that we took Shannon back and killed some of their males in the process."

"They shouldn't have taken her."

"I agree."

"They were going to do some seriously fucked-up shit to her. That's not cool. Only a douchebag would force a woman."

"The prides are angry that we killed them. They also don't know it's mating heat and probably the worst time ever to pull this stunt. Charma came to warn us. She thinks they'll hit town tomorrow but you're not going anywhere without me. That's why you've got to stay inside."

"Fine, but I can handle some pussies."

"They're sending a few dozen and I'm betting they'll stick together. They know we'd win in a fair fight."

"Great." Braden grinned. "I can at least fight if I can't fuck."

"I hear you, man. I was really happy to get the call there was trouble in town."

"You should have taken me with you."

"There wasn't time and besides, you're the baby."

"Screw you." He frowned. "I'm twenty-five years old."

"I know, Braden. That's young. You're still learning how to control your aggression and it's so much worse now. We sometimes need to knock some heads together but you might end up killing someone by accident. Trust me when I say you have no idea how easy it is to lose control."

Braden hesitated. "Your back?"

"My back," he confirmed, turning enough to show his cousin the scars. "This was youth and stupidity. I'm lucky to be alive after taking on that group of rogues. I'd have been dog food if Rave hadn't shown up when he did."

"Fine. Can I at least have more porn flicks?"

"Hang on. I'll grab my favorite five. I kept those for myself." He grinned widely. "I don't need them anymore. I have a mate."

"Fuck you," Braden muttered. "No need to rub it in. I can smell how hot she is and it's torture. I swear I'm going to find a girlfriend before next year so I don't have to go through this heat alone ever again."

"You're too immature to mate."

"I said a girlfriend, not a mate. I don't want one of those until I at least try to have a long-term relationship first."

Brand snorted. "Good luck finding a real girlfriend. The women you spend time with are into screwing almost every guy in our pack and all the surrounding ones. They aren't settle-down types if you want to try your hand at a monogamous relationship.

That stunt you pulled playing stripper wrecked your chances of any serious woman giving you the time of day. You mocked the system by fucking those three women at that party. No one is going to forget that anytime soon."

"They were hot and depressed. I just wanted to cheer them up."

"They were promised to mate guys from other packs but you still had sex with them. You're lucky it didn't get you killed."

"Yeah, but it was really fun and I was right. I can totally handle three women at once." Braden grinned. "And they weren't mated yet. I thought they might enjoy a last fling. I saved them money by providing my body to them at that send-off party. I can dance and strip at the same time. Did you know some guys actually charge money to do that shit? I totally want that job."

"And that's why you're single. It was wrong, Braden. Their families made those alliances, yet you put them at risk. Never touch a woman promised to someone else. You screwed three of them in the same night."

"I did." He grinned, holding up three fingers. "You're just a little jealous that I have that kind of stamina."

"Wrong. You're missing the damn point. You shamed the entire family."

Braden's cheerful expression changed to one of seriousness. "I get it. My bad, but that wasn't my intent. They weren't happy when their parents made those agreements. They didn't love those guys and they wanted to rebel. They needed to have a little fun and I gave them an outlet to do both. Would you have preferred they spent that night crying and being miserable? You're judging something you don't understand."

A hint of pain glimmering in his cousin's gaze surprised Brand. "Talk to me without the usual act you put on for everyone, then. What *did* happen that night besides you fucking them, if it wasn't you just being irresponsible?"

"I knew those girls. They were my friends. They got a raw deal so I showed up at Carmen's house to wish them luck with their new lives. It was just the three of them having a pity party. You can't imagine how much ice cream depressed chicks can put away."

"Ice cream?" Brand hadn't expected that.

"They'd been crying, empty ice cream cartons were all over the coffee table and it broke my heart, man. You should be allowed to mate someone you love, not because your parents were lured by money. That's what it boiled down to. Carmen's old man sold her to the Carlton Pack for a new truck because they're short on women there. Tina and Mandy were traded to the Bolt Pack because they promised their parents a vacation home near a lake and access to the territory. Someone thought it would be cool to mate their twin sons to a set of twin girls. How fucked is that? They had no say in the matter."

124

"It isn't right, but they could have gone to Uncle Elroy and asked him to stop the matings if the girls were dead-set against them."

"My mom ruled on the decisions concerning the girls." Braden looked disgusted. "She made it clear their lives would be hell if they stayed or created waves. She didn't want them around in case I or my brothers took interest in them. They were from poor families, not good enough for her precious boys. I love my mother but she's the ultimate bitch. We wanted to get even and have fun at the same time. Mission accomplished. Now tell me that any family considering trading their daughters for profit won't think about what happened that night and worry about a repeat. We sent a message that no one will forget. It's not acceptable to force matings, and there should be consequences when it happens. I brought shame to my family and they did the same to theirs, which was deserved. That was the damn point, Brand."

Brand understood. He wouldn't have gone to that length to make a point but he respected his cousin on a new level. Payback was something he could relate to. "Were you the one to think up that plan?"

"Mandy did." Braden grinned. "She said their old man would be too afraid to sell off their younger sisters if she and Tina were to set an example of how to throw a proper send-off party. It also gave them some protection, because their new mates would be afraid to hurt them since we'd become intimate friends. Our family is known

125

for kicking some ass to protect the people we care about. Carmen just wanted to piss off her dad, and I could relate. Mom hit the roof. You know how she felt about us doing anything she didn't approve of."

Brand shook his head but was amused. "Your heart and dick were in the right place, huh? I won't bust your balls anymore about that night."

"Speaking of balls, let me go to the runnings. I'll be careful."

"It's too dangerous. Sorry. Hang on while I grab those movies. That's the best I can do for you. And don't enter my room again unless I actually yell for you."

"Got it."

Chapter Six

Charma grinned as Brand held out the spoon. "Seriously?"

He wiggled it in front of her mouth. "Take a bite. You're too thin. I bought chocolate ice cream and brownies. Eat."

"So you put them all together and this is lunch? Really?"

His gaze dropped to her waist. "I miss those curves."

"I'm definitely going to get them back if you keep feeding me this way. This morning I thought the pancakes with chocolate chips and chocolate syrup was over the top, but this is junk food on a whole new level. I'm not a full shifter, you know. My human side is going to pack on the weight."

"Good. You shouldn't be this thin. You need to gain at least forty pounds."

"I really missed you, Brand. Have I said that enough? Most guys want model types. *You* sure don't."

"I want you happy, and you're sexy when you're all curvy and plush. I'm afraid I'm going to break you. I can feel your bones."

The phone rang and he sighed, handing her the utensil. "Hang on. I have to get that."

"Will they be angry about me being here?"

"No. This will concern what to do about the prides."

Charma watched him stride quickly to the wall and answer the phone. She couldn't stare at him enough. Sleeping in his arms had been pure heaven the night before and the amount of sex he needed was over the top. Her muscles ached but she wasn't going to complain.

"Okay." He paused. "Right. I'll be there." He hung up and turned. "That was Rave. He and his brothers are holding a meeting at my uncle's house. A few strangers were spotted on the outer edges of town and from the smell of them, your pride has already reached us. They're probably waiting until darkness falls to attack but just in case, don't leave the house."

"I would be too afraid to do that," she admitted. "I'll never forget last night. I thought those wolves were going to tear me out of the car and rip me to shreds."

Rage twisted his features. "Fuck. That's another thing that's going to be taken care of today. It won't ever happen again, once the pack is informed you're my mate. We have a lot of wolves visiting from nearby areas but they'll immediately take off to avoid being dragged into a war. Word will spread fast that the runnings have been canceled and why."

"What's that?"

He hesitated.

Charma studied him. He obviously didn't want to answer her. "What is a running? Some werewolf thing? Do you shift and all run together?"

"Um..."

The door to the basement jerked open and Braden stepped into the kitchen. He glanced at Charma, grinning. "At this time of year, it's when all the single wolves get naked and fuck like mad in the woods during mating heat." He glanced at his cousin. "I heard your conversation as I came up the stairs. We're going to a pack meeting at Dad's? Is that what you said? I'm dressed and dying to go somewhere. No offense, but your basement is making me claustrophobic."

The information of what a running was settled into Charma and her gaze fixed on Brand. He avoided looking at her, instead glaring at his cousin. It suddenly became clear why he hadn't wanted to answer her question. The image of Brand out there running with a bunch of female wolves to have sex made her lose her appetite. She wondered how many of his pack bitches he knew intimately.

"Yeah," Brand growled. "We're going to your dad's house. Go wait for me in the truck."

Braden frowned. "Why are you angry? You don't want to leave your mate? I get that."

Charma cleared her throat. "I think it's because you just answered a question he was avoiding."

Braden paled. He glanced between her and Brand, inched away from his cousin and winced. "Sorry. You didn't want her to know? Shit." He put more distance between them. "Hey, he hasn't gone in a few years. That's good news, right? He got sick of women coming after him for all the wrong reasons."

"Shut up," Brand rumbled. "Now."

"What?" Braden got closer to Charma, putting her between him and Brand. "I've got your back. She won't be angry if I explain it to her. He's the nephew of the pack alpha, and a lot of women try to lure him into mating to challenge for the leadership of their packs. He inherited the strength of the bloodline and all the traits of an alpha. He's too loyal to our family though, choosing to be an enforcer here rather than killing another alpha to take over a territory. He's a great guy but the women don't care about that. It's just his bloodline they want, and his strength."

"Shut *up*," Brand warned, taking a threatening step forward. "You're digging a hole and don't even know it."

"I'm not! I goofed up and I'm clearing the air. Most women from our pack won't even consider mating with him while my older brothers are single. They're hoping they'll hook up with *them* instead, but other packs would be thrilled to have Brand. He got tired of women trying to use him. That's why he stopped going.

They'd hound him for months afterward if he fucked any of them. He's a prime catch for some bitches."

"Shut up!" Brand snarled, his fangs elongating.

Charma rose from her chair and frowned. "Calm down."

"He's upsetting you."

"I'm fine. You beating on your cousin, though, *will* upset me. I hate to clean up blood."

"I just told her you haven't gone to the runnings in years. He usually holes up with one bitch or hides in his house until mating heat is over. He doesn't even keep a girlfriend for long."

"Shut up." Brand lunged.

Charma stepped into his path and her palms flattened on his chest to hold him in place. She turned her head to shoot Braden a pleading look. "Go wait in the truck and seal your lips."

He fled, the door slamming behind him. Brand's body trembled against her hands as she gave him her full attention. She had to tilt her head back to peer at his face. He grimly regarded her.

"I'm sorry."

She rubbed him. "For what?"

"You shouldn't have heard about that."

"You had sex while we were apart. I'm just grateful you didn't mate anyone. It would break my heart to see you with someone else and not be able to be with you. It worked out, didn't it?"

131

His hands gripped her hips. "You're the only woman I've ever loved, hon."

"You're the only man I've ever loved. It doesn't matter. Your runnings are over though." She smiled to soften her words. "That *would* upset me."

"Never. You're it for me."

"We're fine then."

"I'm your mate. I'd never want another."

She leaned into him and dropped her chin. Her cheek rested against his chest. He hugged her and placed a kiss on top of her head.

"I'm not him."

"I know."

It amazed her that Brand would guess she had thought about Garrett and how he'd cheated. She'd driven him to it but it had still shocked her at first. She hadn't been hurt, though, more relieved that he'd sought out physical release with other women. The thought of Brand touching someone else made pain sear through her heart.

"I'll send Braden without me and stay here with you. They don't really need me at the meeting."

"No. You should go. I'll be fine and this is about your pack. That's important." She pulled away enough to meet his intense gaze. "Call me if you have any questions about the prides. I'd offer to come along but I'm kind of afraid to do that."

"It's *our* pack now, yours too, and after this meeting, you'll be safe anywhere you go within our territory. I'll make damn sure of that and my cousins will back me."

"Are you sure?" It worried her still that his pack might not accept her.

"Positive. Grady married a full human and Anton mated a quarter-puma." He grinned. "Now we have a half-breed spotted leopard in the family. We're going to gain a reputation for being a totally cool pack. All we need now is a bear shifter—and I'm thinking Braden should volunteer for that."

"Don't bears hate *everyone*? I heard stories that they eat our kind."

"Yes." He chuckled. "That's why I think Braden should go find one to bring home. He'll be on toast the first time he pisses her off, which shouldn't take too long."

She laughed, shook her head and pulled out of his arms. "He's young and his intentions were good."

"I'll try to remember that. Lock the door and don't answer it. I'll be back soon. Get the phone if it rings."

"I will."

He leaned down to kiss her lips. "I'll be home real soon. I can't be away for long." He growled softly and a hungry look filled his gaze as it traveled down her body. "I'm already hurting for you."

"I'll eat and wait for you on the bed." She backed away. "Naked."

A pained look crossed his handsome features. "Now I'm really hurting. Damn, hon, don't torment me while I'm in heat. I'll hurry. Lock the door." He spun on his heel and left the house.

* * * * *

Brand shot dirty looks at Braden the entire trip to the Harris Pack alpha's house. "You don't speak to my mate of such things," he ordered.

"I'm sorry." His cousin shifted a little closer to the door to keep space between them. "Where's your sense of humor? Gaining a mate has made you kind of a dick."

"You could have hurt her feelings. I didn't want her to know about the runnings. It's not cool to discuss fucking other women in front of your mate."

"She would have heard the truth from someone at some point. She didn't seem angry."

"You're lucky." Brand slowed the truck and parked behind a line of vehicles near the driveway. "Just don't talk when you're around her."

134

"Really? I'm living in your basement."

Brand growled softly. "Fine. Just don't discuss sex with her, or bitches, and take hints when I shoot a glare your way. That means shut your trap."

"I'm sure cats have runnings."

"You'd be wrong." Brand jerked on the handle and slid out of his truck. "The females can take pills to stop the heat. They only allow it to happen when they're with someone they trust or when they're already mated. It's frowned upon if they get pregnant otherwise."

"Tell it to those pussies who wanted to hurt Shannon."

"Only prides with low birthrates are willing to do that breeding-for-litters bullshit, and from what I've heard, they force the half-breed mothers to give up those babies to barren full-blooded women to raise."

"That's some fucked-up shit."

"Agreed. Just watch your mouth around Charma and remember that she's different from us."

"Fine."

They walked side by side to the front door. Braden opened it and stalked inside first. The scent of pack filled the entire house and it didn't surprise Brand that they'd met in the large living room instead of going downstairs where they held their usual family meetings. He nodded at his packmates but ignored the shocked

135

expressions as they got a whiff of him. He'd expected the scent of Charma to draw plenty of attention.

Rave met his gaze across the room. He watched his cousin sniff the air and a grin spread across his face. "Glad you dragged your ass out of bed."

Grady walked out of the kitchen with a beer in his hand. His head snapped in Brand's direction and then his eyebrows lifted.

"Charma came home to me."

"The spotted leopard from college?" A smile curved Grady's lips. "I heard something about her from Rave."

"She's not leaving me a second time." He lifted his chin to level a fierce look at the faces around the room. "She's my mate. Got it? Anyone have a problem with that? Say so now and I'll kill you before the meeting starts."

"We welcome your mate, so don't slaughter anyone." Anton's deep voice spoke as he entered the room carrying a big tray of food. "Congratulations. Tell her thanks for the heads-up on the pride threat." He shot a menacing look around the room. "Is everyone cool with she-cats as protected mates in our pack? If not, step outside to get your ass kicked. You can pick who you want to fight but there will be no killings. I'd hate to get stains on Dad's carpet so we will definitely take it to the backyard. There's a hose out there to wash away the blood."

No one spoke or moved toward the door.

Brand relaxed. He'd never worried that his cousins would have a problem with Charma, but the other wolves were another matter. Some of them were older, set in their ways, and cats were considered to be the enemy, no exceptions made. He had a suspicion that some weren't cool with it but they were too afraid to protest. They'd get their asses handed to them by a Harris family member.

Anton placed the tray on the coffee table and moved to sit in a chair by the fireplace, apparently relaxed. Brand knew better. His cousin's eyes were solemn, his fingers clawed a little on the arms of the chair. Brand took a seat on the couch opposite him.

"We have pride males lurking outside of town and they think they can take us." Anton leaned forward a little. His cold smile didn't reach his eyes and his voice was gruff. "The runnings are officially canceled. Spread the word to your family and neighbors. Any visitors we have need to leave. It's too dangerous to be caught unaware that way. I want them gone, even if they offer to stay. The last thing we need is other packs pissed that they lost some of their own in our war. Turn your cell phones on and keep them close. I'm ordering families to go into house lockdown. The more family members in one home, the better. If you scent cat, call for help. We'll be there with the enforcers immediately."

Raymond Borl protested. "I don't want my son-by-mate fucking my daughter under my roof. That's why they have their own home."

137

"Would you prefer to hear she was killed when they were slaughtered at their home?" Grady crossed his arms over his chest. "We're better off staying in large numbers since I'm sure those pride males will attack en masse. They would be stupid to separate into smaller groups to come at us."

"What if you're attacked inside your home with no one else there, Raymond?" Braden snorted. "Bob is a good fighter, and you'd want him at your side to defend his mate *and* yours until help reached you."

The older wolf rose to his feet and bared his teeth. "This wouldn't be an issue if your family hadn't attacked a pride. You invaded their territory first, not the other way around. You brought this on us!"

Anton moved so fast that Raymond didn't even have time to flinch before he landed on his ass after being punched. "*They* invaded our territory first to take my mate. They had no right to come here."

The older man on the floor coughed, rubbing his injured chest. "Your mother invited them to take that she-cat back where she belonged. They had her permission to cross into our territory."

Rave grabbed his brother's arm and hauled Anton back. "Easy," he hissed, shooting a glare around the room. "Our mother had *no* authority to allow them here, and she has been banned from our pack for treachery against her own family. She's paying for her crimes. Her mate shunned her. That she-cat you're speaking of is a

Harris now, a member of this pack, and considered one of us. This is where she belongs. Anyone who betrays this pack will face the same fate as my mother. She gave birth to me but I packed her bags myself. Remember that, if you think you're immune from our wrath just because we've known you all our lives. This isn't a democracy. Your acting alpha just gave you an order."

Braden inched closer, shooting Brand a meaningful glance. It reminded him that he was usually the one who calmed tensions at pack meetings, often with his humor. He didn't have any at the moment where prides or the pack's stance on she-cats mated to werewolves were concerned. It affected Charma. It wasn't a joking matter that someone thought they shouldn't be defended because they weren't bitches.

He stood, knowing he needed to say something.

"You can whine about why this happened later," he stated gruffly. "Right now our pack is in danger. The pride males are going to be looking for small groups of us to attack but we won't give them that." Something his mate said surfaced in Brand's memory. "We're a pack. We stick together and back each other up. We work well together as one unit." He stepped forward and bent, offering a hand to Raymond. "They are pride. They fight amongst themselves and won't be able to spend much time together. Let's show them why we're to be feared—unity."

Raymond took his hand and Brand pulled him to his feet. He released the jerk as soon as he could and resisted the urge to knock him back on his ass. Brand glanced around the room, looking for more trouble, but didn't see it.

"You've got your orders," Anton growled. "Move out. Enforcers, stay."

The room cleared. Brand waited until the door closed before he frowned at Anton. "Where's Von?" His cousin wasn't present, something he'd taken note of when he arrived. It concerned him. Anton, Rave, Grady, Von and Braden always backed each other up. It was odd that one would miss a mandatory pack meeting.

Grady ran his fingers through his hair. "We don't know."

"What do you mean, you don't know?" Braden's alarm was evident. "Did those damn cats grab him?"

Anton closed the distance and gripped his youngest brother's shoulders. "He's fine. He called my cell and left a message early this morning. He said something came up. It was an emergency and he had to leave town for a few days. He used the safe word. He wouldn't have done that if someone forced him to make the call. The pride doesn't have him."

Now worry hit Brand hard. "Didn't he hook up with someone for mating heat? Is she with him?"

"He had Debbie staying at his house," Kane, the pack's lead enforcer, explained. "He didn't take her with him. He called and had me go tell her how sorry he was for leaving. I escorted her to her parents' after stopping at a store on the way." He actually blushed. "She needed some supplies."

"Supplies?" Braden cocked his head. "What? They didn't have enough food?"

Anton chuckled and released his brother to smack the side of his head. "She's in heat too. I'm thinking what Kane isn't saying is she needed lots of batteries for her vibrator."

Rave chuckled. "He blushes."

Kane flipped him off. "Screw you. It was uncomfortable, okay? She's like a kid sister to me." He stared at Anton. "Von refused to tell me where he was going or what he needed to do. I'm worried."

"Me too." Anton frowned, glancing around the room. "Does anyone know anything?"

Silence reigned.

Anton studied Kane. "You were on duty with him last night. Did something happen?"

"Nothing weird. We picked up the scent of a couple of humans by the pack graveyard. Von said he'd deal with scaring them off and sent me home." His cheeks colored slightly again. "The heat was getting to me. I was sweating bad and he told me to go take care of business. He was fine when I left him. He'd taken some drugs to dull the desire. He said someone should keep a clear head, considering the state of the pack. Tension is high since your father shunned your mother and had to go on medical leave to survive cutting the bond with his mate."

"Fuck," Rave groaned. "It has to be something major for him to take off while in heat without one of our women with him to keep him sane. How bad does it have to be for him not to tell us what's up?"

"Call him," Braden demanded.

"We have," Grady offered. "Many times. He's not picking up and it goes straight to voice mail. I have no idea what's up but right now we have other shit to deal with."

"Nothing is more important than finding Von," Rave growled.

"You think I don't feel the same?" Grady held his gaze. "We're all worried but he's tough enough to handle himself."

"Grady is right." Anton sighed. "We'll deal with finding Von later. Right now we need to protect the pack. Von had no idea of the seriousness of the threat we're under or he'd be here. We left messages so hopefully he'll hear them and show up soon."

"This is a cluster-fuck," Braden groaned. "Von is missing and we've got a pride about to attack."

"We'll handle those pussies and then track down Von." Rave glanced at his brothers. "Where are we staying?"

"Here," Anton announced. "It's big enough to house all of us. The enforcers are taking over the basement and you've got an hour to grab your stuff. I expect everyone to return by then."

"Fuck no," Rave rumbled. "I refuse to share a house with over twenty people."

"Deal with it. We need to set an example," Anton reminded him. "So far you haven't done a good job of that after we ordered everyone to double up. You said Braden drove you nuts and you sent him to Brand. You demanded Shannon and I move to Grady's place. We're alpha-blooded, two of us could fight off a few dozen pride members. The rest of the pack wouldn't stand a chance against those numbers so we'll bring the fight to us. It's best if we're all under one roof. We'll be their main target so we may as well make it easy for them to find us." He grinned. "And this is the first place they'll look. Rave can find some humans to fill in at the bar and make sure they know where to send anyone who comes looking for a Harris."

"Done." Rave nodded.

"Rave drove *me* nuts," Braden muttered. "Not the other way around. He took over Anton's old schedule of the prospective out-of-town mates. Do you know what it was like, hearing him nailing different women every few hours that first night? He took them to the guestroom right next to mine." He flipped off his brother. "Just to rub it in so I'd know exactly what they were doing."

"Shut up," Rave growled. "I didn't want their scent in my bedroom. I had to listen to you whine constantly about how mean it was to smell sex when you couldn't get laid."

143

"I could if I hadn't been banned by Dad from touching pack women!"

Grady stepped between them. "Rave, stop needling him, and Braden, you're happier with Brand. It's your *own* fault you were banned from fucking pack women unless you got a serious girlfriend. You damn near caused three males to kill you when you crashed that party. Those women's future mates weren't amused when they'd discovered you'd nailed them."

"I *was* happy at Brand's house," he corrected. "But now I have to listen to him doing his mate. And you would have done what I did too. I just offered up my bod to three women who wanted one last fling. Those weren't love matches."

Kane groaned. "I'm the one who had to talk their future mates out of killing your ass the morning after when they arrived to pick up those women. You were passed out from exhaustion when the shitstorm hit."

Braden grinned. "Thanks."

Kane glared. "I can't wait until you mature. Like I don't have enough to do without cleaning up your messes."

"Let's change the subject," Brand suggested, wanting to save Braden some grief.

"I agree. Enough," Anton softly ordered. "You've all got one hour to pack a bag, grab whoever you're spending your heat with and get back here. We're going on lockdown until this is over." He stared at Kane. "Patrols go out in shifts, with two of us and enforcers, no less than eight-member teams at a time. That's how it's going to be until the pride realizes they can't win. I refuse to lose anyone on my watch while our father is down. I gave him my word we'd take care of everyone, and that means nobody dies."

"Easier said than done," Kane muttered. "But agreed. We stick together while we're out and everyone stays ready to roll if trouble hits. I'll call my brother. He took the night shift but he's slept for at least four hours by now."

Brand sighed. "Great. It's going to be damn crowded here. I just took a mate."

"So did I." Anton gave him a sympathetic look. "Protecting them takes priority over privacy right now."

"Is Dad safe? He can't defend himself while he's drugged. Maybe we should wake him." Braden seemed nervous.

"He's stashed with the doctor. The prides won't find him, and I assigned three elder, trusted enforcers to stand guard," Anton informed him. "We can't risk waking him until after heat. The severed mate bond would kill him for sure at this time. The best chance he has of surviving is being kept in an induced coma."

"We've got this," Grady confirmed. "Dad's safer where he is."

"What about my fucking schedule?" Rave arched his eyebrows. "I have appointments booked with those bitches from other packs. Do I just have them come here?"

"I'll call their packs to cancel the meetings. I'm sure their fathers won't want to send them into a battle zone just on the off chance that you'll pick one of them to mate. I know they want a Harris to add to their bloodline but they want their daughters alive more." Anton shrugged. "It's too dangerous for them to be here, and I don't want a pack war on top of it if one of them were to die when a fight breaks out."

"Then who am I supposed to fuck?" A horrified look crossed Rave's face.

Braden snickered. "Your hand. It isn't so funny when it's being said to *you*, is it? I suggest you stop at a store and buy a dozen bottles of lotion. You'll want the oily kind."

Rave opened his mouth to speak but his cell phone rang, halting whatever response he was about to make. He grabbed it but shot a menacing glare at his baby brother before leaving the room to answer. "It's my shop. I have to take this."

"Let's go." Anton sighed. "We'll kick some ass hard and fast so this ends quickly. I don't know how I'm going to tell Shannon about our new living arrangements but it's necessary. She had a hard enough time not being embarrassed having one of my brothers within hearing range of us in bed. Now she's going to have an entire houseful to deal with."

Brand said nothing but he hated the idea of subjecting Charma to so many werewolves too. She wasn't used to them and he wasn't sure how she'd react. Keeping her protected was paramount

146

though. She'd be safer with plenty of pack to guard the house while he worked his patrol shifts.

Rave returned, his face grim. "Some bitch showed up at my shop. It has to be my two o'clock appointment arriving a bit early, but she mustn't have gotten the address I texted her. At least I'll get in one last fuck before I return. I'll make a few calls about the bar too. It will be handled."

"An hour," Anton warned. "One. Make it a quickie and send her home, damn it. Don't bring her back. I mean it about not wanting them endangered if shit hits the fan. Those women are alpha-blooded and their packs would take serious offense if we allowed her to stay in a war zone."

"Got it." Rave sailed out the front door.

Brand turned and motioned to Braden that it was time to leave. He wanted to get back to Charma. He missed her and hated leaving her alone.

Chapter Seven

The phone rang and Charma rolled over on the bed to reach for the receiver on the nightstand. "Hello?"

There was a pause. "I'm sorry. I must have dialed the wrong number."

The other woman sounded perky and young. "Were you looking for Brand? He's not home right now."

"Who is this?" The tone changed from friendly to downright hostile.

A stab of jealousy pierced her heart for a second and suspicion flared that the person on the other end of the line was someone Brand had been seeing before her arrival. She was torn between the satisfaction of being able to claim Brand as her mate and knowing the right thing to do would be to allow him to be the one to share that news.

"I'm Charma. Would you like to leave a message?"

"Did he hook up with you during the heat? Goddamn it!" The woman snarled. "That bastard. He was supposed to meet up with me in the woods yesterday but never showed. I just heard the runnings were called off so I assumed he wasn't able to make it because of the trouble they said is heading our way."

Charma winced, her suspicion confirmed. She wasn't sure what to say, so remained silent.

"I don't recognize your voice." The woman was worked up, her voice angry. "But let me tell you something about Brand Harris. He's a cold son of a bitch without a heart. He'll use you and toss you away as soon as some fresh meat hits town. Ask any woman in the pack and they'll tell you how sorry you'll be if you think he's a keeper."

That pissed Charma off. "Brand is a wonderful, loving man."

The woman snorted loudly. "Right. You keep saying that until you realize it's just sex to him. You think you're the first bitch he's fooled into thinking he'd be a great mate? I could give you a list of people to call who'd tell you the truth. Don't get too comfortable, bitch. Your ass will be booted out of the territory as soon as the heat is over. He's a user."

That was it. No one insulted her mate. "What's your name?"

"I'm Peggy. Did I mention he hates kids? What kind of jerk does that? He's nothing like Alpha Elroy. Now that's a *real* man who values taking care of his pack and has a sense of honor. He should banish his nephew and do this entire pack a favor."

"I wanted to give Brand the chance to break this to you gently but you don't seem the nice type who deserves that respect, since you show none for him. Brand is my *mate*. He loves me. How dare you try to spread the garbage you just spewed? I know him better

149

than you *ever* did if you actually believe that bullshit. He's very loving, very kind, and he reeks of honor. He also loves children. He's always wanted to have them with me. Did you ever consider if he's cold to you, it might be because you're a nasty, spiteful bitch? I'll tell him you called." She slammed the phone down.

Charma closed her eyes and cursed. She hadn't handled that well. The phone rang again and she gritted her teeth. She lifted the receiver. "Hello?" She had a sinking feeling it would be Peggy calling back. She wasn't wrong.

"He mated you?"

"Yes." Charma took a deep breath and opened her eyes, staring at the ceiling. "We go way back. I just arrived in town last night."

"And he *mated* you?" Peggy gasped.

"We're as mated as a couple can be."

"Son of a bitch! That bastard! That rat! That—"

"I've heard enough. I'll tell Brand you called. Please don't call back. I don't want to hear any more." Charma hung up.

The phone didn't ring a third time. She rolled out of bed and entered Brand's bathroom, grabbing his robe off the hook. It smelled of him. She decided to go search the kitchen for some chocolate. Brand loved the stuff so she felt certain she'd find a hidden stash somewhere.

The front door opened as she crossed the living room and Brand walked in. He grinned, his gaze raking her from head to foot.

"I thought you were going to wait for me in bed?" He closed and locked the door behind him. He moved purposefully, his intent to take her to bed obvious.

She held up a hand. "Give me a few minutes." She fled into the kitchen.

Brand followed. "What's wrong?"

"Nothing," she lied, opening his pantry. "Where's your candy bar stash?"

"Top right, behind the cereal boxes. Hon, what's wrong? You're tense."

He knew her well, but she knew him too. She found the box. It was nearly full. Her wolf had always loved his chocolate. She removed two candy bars and spun, holding one out to him.

"You had a phone call while you were gone. Peggy is very upset. I'm sorry but she said some bad things about you that set me off. I told her we were mated, and I'm pretty sure I wasn't real kind about it."

His expression twisted into a grimace. "Shit. It's not what you think. I've never slept with her."

That surprised Charma. "She's angry that you didn't meet her yesterday."

"She set that up but I never agreed." He tossed the candy bar on the counter then stalked closer, boxed her into the corner and snagged hers to send it flying across the room. "Don't let her upset

151

you. She lost her mate last year and was trying to talk me into taking on her and her nine pups."

"Nine? She sounded so young."

"She mated at eighteen and now she's thirty. Dan pretty much kept her pregnant because she wanted a ton of kids. He was a good guy, but had bad taste in women. She's kind of annoying with her hyper personality."

Guilt struck. "Her mate died? That's awful."

"Yeah. It was. She'd asked my cousin to stop serving him drinks at his place, so he went to a bar out of our territory and ended up taking on some rogues in a fight. He lost his life. We tracked them down and dealt with the ones responsible." He flattened his palms on the wall to keep her in place but didn't touch her. "I'm sorry she upset you."

"I was more angry than hurt. She said some terrible things about you that weren't true."

"That's Peggy. She's kind of immature and tends to blow everything out of proportion when she doesn't get her way. Are you okay?" He paused. "Are *we* okay? I never touched her."

She stared into his eyes, knowing he spoke the truth. She stepped into him until she pressed against his body. "Why would she say such horrible things about you?"

He frowned. "What did she say?"

"You hate kids, you're coldhearted. She pretty much made you sound like a jerk."

"I told you that you're the only one I've ever loved, hon. Some women see me as heartless. I don't hate kids. I just didn't want to take on her nine pups."

"You offered to love any children I had."

"That's because they would have been a part of *you*. Peggy wanted a pup wrangler and she sure as hell doesn't love me. She likes my bank account."

"Your bank account?"

"I do well in real estate."

That surprised her. "You were going to become the accountant for your pack."

"Things changed after you left. I doubled my classes to finish my degree but I just couldn't stand to be there without you." His big hands gently wrapped around her hips. "I discovered I love tearing shit apart so I started flipping houses. You know. Buying rundown properties and fixing them up to sell at a much higher price. I started my own company and have done well. I'm not rich by some standards but we're financially stable. I also help the pack as an enforcer. We get a salary for that because it can take up a lot of hours, depending on the time of year."

"Like when you guys go into mating heat?"

"Exactly." His voice deepened. "Speaking of which, I need you."

She forgot about the candy bars. She gripped Brand's shoulders and jumped, wrapping her legs around his waist. "Take me to the bedroom. I don't want your cousin catching us again. Is he here?"

"Yeah." Brand cupped her ass, carrying her out of the kitchen. "He's downstairs packing."

"He's leaving?"

He hesitated. "We'll talk about that at the alpha house later. I must have you right now."

He dropped her on the bed, turned and tried to close the busted door. A frustrated growl tore from him when the broken doorjamb prevented it from closing. One punch and the jamb snapped off. The door closed completely and he moved to the dresser, dragging it over as reinforcement, to effectively make sure they weren't disturbed. He turned and hastily removed his shirt.

Charma removed his robe and tossed it to the floor, then took a seat. Desire darkened Brand's gaze, which was locked on her breasts. She leaned back and centered her body on the mattress. It warmed her to feel so desired by Brand. He kicked off his boots and shoved down his jeans. She smiled at the sight of his stiff erection and licked her lips.

Brand advanced. "Don't even tease. I can't let you do that."

Her gaze lifted. "I miss tasting you."

154

He climbed on the bed, his hungry stare taking in every inch of her from head to toe. "I miss your mouth wrapped around my cock too. You have no damn idea how many times I tormented myself with that memory but I'm too out of control. I need to be inside you, and I won't be all that gentle once I am."

She reached for him, sliding her palms over his firm chest. "Is that supposed to scare me?"

"Nope. It's just a warning. Roll over and get on your knees."

"I'm not ready," she admitted. "No foreplay?"

"We have to be at the alpha house in less than an hour. I'll get you wet but I want you on all fours right now."

Questions surfaced but he wasn't in the mood to talk. She stopped exploring his rib cage with her fingers and rolled onto her stomach. He moved back as she lifted to her hands and knees.

"Spread wide for me."

She parted her legs farther and Brand made an animalistic sound. She lowered her head and waited, hoping he wouldn't just take her. Her body wasn't prepared.

He fixed that by stretching out on his back, gripping her hips, and settling her spread thighs directly over his face. His hot, wet mouth located her clit.

Her nails dug into the bed. She'd forgotten how he sometimes didn't bother with formalities like kissing her lips or even bothering to tell her what he was about to do. Her mate growled, sending vibrations to that sensitive bundle of nerves as he used his tongue. Teeth raked gently over it, too, and she threw her head back.

"Fuck, baby," she panted. "Slow down. It's too intense."

He ignored her, focusing on one spot that drove her out of her mind. It was as if he was determined to make her come fast and hard. She tried to jerk away because the pleasure was too raw and intense but his hands clenched, holding her in place with no way to escape. Her muscles tensed and she gave in, not fighting. The climax tore through her with a brutal force that left her crying out, without the ability to even form words.

His hands released her, she was aware of that much, and the mattress shifted under her as he moved. She would have fallen over from the motion but his arm hooked around her waist before she lost her balance and his cock nudged the entrance to her pussy. He drove in deep with one fluid thrust, his thick shaft forcing her muscles to part and accept him. He dropped down to curve around her and used his free hand to brace on the bed beside one of hers.

"You're wet *now*," he snarled.

There was no denying that. Brand pounded her, fucking her deep. He was rock hard, thick, and moved fast enough that she had no chance of matching his pace. A new kind of pleasure began building, until she knew she was about to come again. Time lost meaning as she cried out, her mind blown a second time.

Brand clenched his teeth to avoid sinking them into Charma's exposed shoulder. Her throaty moans and the sound of her coming sent him over the edge. He drove in deep, his body seizing as his semen blasted out, filling his mate. *Heaven. That's where she takes me every time we make love.*

He almost snorted at the term when he stopped coming and could think straight again. He had her pinned under him and he eased his hold on her waist to make sure she wasn't being crushed. *That wasn't making love.* Guilt struck next. She deserved tenderness from him, not what he'd just done.

"Was I too rough?"

She tossed her hair and looked back at him. Her smile alleviated any apprehension. His hand massaged her, since he wasn't willing to pull his dick out of her, happy to keep them joined at the hips.

"I've got nothing to complain about."

He didn't agree. "Sorry."

Her smile faded. "Don't. If you didn't notice, I enjoyed that a lot."

"I just screwed you, when I should have taken my time and met more of your needs instead of just my own."

"They were met." She wiggled her ass and tried to move out from under him.

Regretfully, he lifted up, allowing her to go. "I just missed you and hadn't planned to be gone so long." It was a lousy excuse but it was the truth.

She rolled over and sat, peering steadfastly into his eyes. "I like it when you get down and dirty sometimes."

His chest tightened and he knew it was caused by the unbounded love he felt for her. "Is that what you called *that*?"

She laughed and pointed a finger at her lap. "You went down, and then when you were going at me, you were saying dirty words."

He leaned forward and she flattened on the bed to allow him to ease down on top of her. He was careful to distribute his weight so she could breathe easily and continue to catch her breath. "I love you, Charma."

She wrapped her arms around his neck and kissed his lips with a brush of her own. "I love you too."

"I just worry that I'm going to screw this up somehow. I can't take coming home to an empty house a second time."

"You know I didn't leave because of anything you did. You can't get rid of me now. I'm here to stay."

He prayed that was true. "The only reason I survived when you disappeared was because my family kept pulling my ass out of bad situations. I turned self-destructive. You know how I mentioned that I figured out I loved remodeling? I went into rages sometimes

158

and nearly destroyed this place. I had to fix it at some point. That's when I discovered I enjoyed the work."

Her finger slid into his hair and she clenched them, getting a firm enough hold that it stung his scalp. "Listen to me. It wasn't your fault."

"We fought that morning and I shouldn't have stormed out. I just left you when I should have stayed to work it out. I've kicked my own ass over that decision a million times. I drove you to leave."

"People argue, Brand. Just because you love someone doesn't mean you have to agree on everything. It ripped me to shreds when I packed my bag and drove away. It had nothing to do with you going for a run. That was your way of cooling off and I've always understood that. I just realized how much not being mated was tearing us apart. I wouldn't have been able keep saying no if we'd had more time together but I couldn't live with knowing what it would cost my family. I'm the one who's sorry. I should have told you everything but I was too afraid."

"Why?"

She chewed on her bottom lip and he remembered what that meant.

"Spit it out, hon. I hate when you think something but won't share it with me. That's part of the reason you just said you left me. Tell me."

She released her lip and sighed. "You tended to be rash back then. I was terrified you'd make death threats to my pride leader, trying to protect my family from his wrath. I could see you doing that."

"It might have worked."

"You would have been killed, Brand. Percy is a dick, and he would have killed my family out of spite just because you threatened him. He'd have ordered my people to attack you. One wolf against an entire pride is suicide."

"I would have called him out if that were the case. I'd have issued a challenge."

"You're assuming Percy has honor. He has *none*. He rules through fear and intimidation. You would have been facing down every enforcer while he sat on his lazy ass, watching them tear you apart. He'd never have taken you on by himself. He and his son have that in common. They always have others do the dirty work."

Questions filled Brand's head, ones he wasn't sure he wanted answers to, but he had to know. "Did that son of a bitch you mated ever allow anyone else to hurt you, Charma?"

"No. He did that himself. I was weaker and not a threat. He didn't hit me as much as you might assume. We avoided each other most of the time."

He silently swore to hunt the bastard down and kill him after the mating heat passed. He'd seen the bruises on her. It never should have happened. The prick would pay dearly for daring to lay an abusive hand on his Charma.

"I wasn't implying Garrett had others hurt me. I was thinking about what he'd have done to you if you'd shown up on our pride lands. Percy would have had you killed, but Garrett would have made sure you suffered first, Brand. He would have taken it out on you that I'd allowed someone else to touch me."

"You said you weren't dating anyone when we met."

"He wasn't my boyfriend. I never dated him or let him touch me. He tried plenty of times but I wasn't interested. He decided I was going to become his mate and made it clear he'd hurt anyone who looked at me twice. He would have seen it as a betrayal to find out we'd lived together and I loved you. I used to have nightmares about the horrible things he and his friends would have done to you."

Anger rose but he pushed it down. "He might have changed his mind about wanting you for a mate if he'd learned about me."

She eased her hold on his hair. "No, Brand. You don't get it. He *knew* I hated him, that he was the last person I wanted to be with, but he didn't give a damn. He was a spoiled-rotten first son of a pride leader. A bully. Vicious." She took a deep breath. "He beat on and harassed anyone he didn't like because he could. His father never reined him in or scolded him for the messed-up things he did. He just would have made an example of you and counted it as a

161

bonus to watch me suffer your loss. That's the type of jerk he's always been."

"I would have killed him."

"I'm not insulting you. You're obviously a great fighter. I saw that firsthand when you got all those werewolves away from my car, but you would have been facing off against an entire pride. Garrett makes sure he can win before he gets involved. He'd have had his friends attack until you were so injured you couldn't fight back, and then he would have struck."

"I really want him dead."

"So do I."

He studied her closely and saw sincerity. "How could you stand to be with him?" He had a new sense of her inner strength if her life had been as appalling as he suspected.

She looked away. "No choice. I had to stick it out until my sisters were old enough to mate." She held his gaze then. "It was my responsibility as the oldest to keep them safe. I never suspected that one of them would hook up with the son of another pride leader. If she hadn't, I'd still be trapped there until Bree is settled."

The tears that filled her eyes broke his heart but she blinked them away. His mate was strong and beautiful. "I understand. I'd do damn near anything for blood."

"I have." Her smile appeared forced. "Let's change the subject. You said something about us going to the alpha house. Does your family want to meet me?"

It was a reminder that they needed to leave. "My cousin Anton decided it would be safer if the family and the enforcers move into Uncle Elroy's home. We're stronger united, and we're the ones the pride males want. It's safer for our pack if the pride isn't tearing apart the town seeking us out. We'll make certain they know where to come."

She gaped at him.

"It's a good plan. We want to draw them away from the weaker members. There's nothing to worry about. You'll be safe inside the house. I wouldn't leave you here alone anyway. Some of them might decide to go house to house searching for easy prey. My cousins need me in this fight. I wouldn't do it, though, if I believed you'd be in danger. You're my priority."

"You need to fight. I understand that, even if I hate it. I'd never ask you to abandon your family when they're depending on you."

He hadn't thought for a minute she would. She'd suffered plenty for the safety of her own family. "I know it's going to be difficult being around so many wolves but they're aware that you're my mate. No one will dare give you any shit. My cousins and I made that damn clear."

"What about Alpha Elroy? Is he upset that I'm here?"

"No." Brand tried to hide his anguish. "He doesn't know about you. Long story short, his parents arranged his mating to my aunt Eve. He did his best to love her and be a good mate. It wasn't reciprocated. She did something really bad recently and he banished her from our territory. He had no choice but to shun her."

Charma's eyebrows arched, her surprise clear.

"She endangered her own son, put his new mate in grave jeopardy, and planned to kill Uncle Elroy and his half-human son, who was born before they mated. She deserved to die but my uncle has a big heart. Mating heat had begun so losing her at this time would have driven him insane. You don't come back from that. Our doctor put him in an induced coma. My cousins are leading the pack until it's safe to wake him, after the heat passes. He'll have a rough time of it, adjusting to the loss of a mate but he's strong. He'll survive."

She was silent for long moments and seemed to carefully consider what he said. "Will he have a problem with me once he's back in charge?"

"No. He's a good man. As I said, he has a half-human son. He didn't know about Grady until the mother abandoned him on Elroy's doorstep after discovering he could shift. Eve demanded he kill my cousin, but he refused. Grady mated a human. My cousin Anton is the one who mated a she-cat. Uncle Elroy accepted them. He'll accept you too."

She still didn't appear convinced.

"He will, Charma. Uncle Elroy has been a father to me since my parents left."

"You never talked about them except to say they were gone. I thought you meant they'd died. Are they still alive?"

He shrugged. "I don't know. It's not a good story to tell." Charma peered at him until he gave in. He'd do anything for her. "My dad was kind of stupid and thought he'd make a better alpha of this pack. He challenged Uncle Elroy and lost."

That stunned Charma. "I thought werewolves didn't do that kind of thing if they were brothers. Was your mother the sibling to the alpha?"

"Nope. It was my dad. Uncle Elroy should have killed him. That's pretty much a given when you challenge for leadership. They were asked to leave the territory instead and banned from ever coming back."

"How horrible." She massaged his arm. "I'm so sorry, Brand. Why didn't you go with them?"

"My father was wrong. Uncle Elroy is a fantastic pack leader. I was given the choice to stay or go. I chose. My parents were angry, and haven't contacted me since."

"Oh, Brand." Her sadness showed in her eyes.

"Don't feel sorry for me, hon. My cousins are like brothers to me. I might have lost my parents but I kept the whole of my family intact by staying. I've never regretted that. This is my pack."

"But it's got to be hard not knowing where your parents are, or if they're still alive."

"They'd have contacted me if they wanted to. I'm listed in the book. It's not my favorite subject, so let's change it. You asked how I know my uncle will accept you. I know him well, and he's going to welcome you with open arms. I have no doubt about that."

"I'm glad you're so sure." She braved a smile.

"It's going to work out. We need to get ready to leave. We're expected at the alpha house soon."

"I don't have any spare clothes so this shouldn't take long."

"We'll go shopping once the pride males leave town. For now, you can borrow anything of mine you like." He enjoyed the idea of her wearing his stuff but naked was better. His dick hardened. He groaned, glancing down at it with disgust. "We need to hurry before I lose my mind needing you again."

Chapter Eight

Charma stared openly at the attic space that had been converted into a guestroom. The smell of dust tickled her nose. Brand hovered behind her and she turned, catching the worried expression on his face.

"I'm so sorry about this. It's not exactly nice, and I doubt anyone has stayed in this room since Aunt Margie spent the summer five years ago. She had a thing for living in attics after a flood destroyed her home. The higher above ground, the better. I picked it because it's the most private and gives us the floor to ourselves."

"It's great." She glanced at the queen bed, two nightstands and a line of boxes piled up along a wall. "I wish it had a television but there are books." She pointed. "See? Those are clearly marked as romances in that top box to the far left. I love them, so I'll have plenty to read."

He inched closer. "This wasn't how I thought it would be when we mated. It's safer here with all of us under one roof though. I'll get you a TV."

She grinned and stepped into his arms. "I was teasing. With you in heat, I'm sure I'll be far from bored. I don't care where we are as long as we're together. The place just needs a good cleaning."

A soft growl rumbled from him. "I want you."

She pressed her hand against the front of his jeans, caressing the hard length of his cock trapped inside them. Her breasts flattened against his chest. "I'm all yours."

He brushed a kiss over her mouth. "I'll never get tired of hearing you say that. It's not real yet. I keep half expecting to wake up alone to discover none of this was real. It would kill me."

"I'm real." She reached up to dig her fingernails into his biceps. "Feel me."

His arms tightened around her. He lifted her and carried her to the bed. They fell in a heap and dust rose around them, causing both of them to sneeze. A snarl tore from Brand.

"Damn it! This isn't exactly romantic."

Charma chuckled as she slid her fingers into his silky hair. "It doesn't matter. We could be lost in the woods, starving, and it could be pouring rain. I'm happy that I have you."

"I just want everything to be perfect."

She gazed deep into his beautiful eyes. "It is. You're here with me."

He took possession of her mouth again as he shoved her clothing out of the way. She tore at his shirt, attempting to push it up his torso. She needed to feel his skin against hers. The urge to lick him, rake her nails down his back, and the ache between her thighs assured her she was ready to have his cock buried deep inside her.

He was her mate, her life, and every bit of happiness that she'd ever dreamed of having. They were together and nothing else mattered. She was going to enjoy every moment to make up for all the years they'd lost.

Brand rolled over and Charma sat up to straddle his lap. She hooked her fingers beneath her shirt and tore it up her body. His fingers snagged the cups of her bra and tugged to get her breasts free. She unfastened the back of it, wiggled her shoulders and he threw it to the floor. He massaged her taut nipples while she ground her ass over his thighs, wishing they were naked and he was already inside her.

"You're so beautiful. I missed you so much."

Brand's words were enough to make her tear up. "I love you. I died a little every day that we were apart."

He rolled them again to pin her under him and stared deeply into her eyes. "If you ever take off again, I'll track you down, hon. I swear I will. To the ends of the Earth if that's what it takes. I'll never be without you again."

The material ripped as she desperately sought hot skin. "Good. I'll hold you to that promise but I'm not going anywhere. I'm right where I belong."

A growl tore from his throat that promised he wouldn't be gentle fucking her and her excitement level spiked higher. Memories of the past blurred with the present as they kissed. All those years had passed but the strong passion between them hadn't faded. If anything, they'd both learned loss and the value of being together.

His mouth devoured hers as she met his tongue with her own. Charma ground her body against his, needing to feel him. A soft growl came from her throat and surprised them both. Brand responded by snarling. His hands became rougher, gripping her tightly, and he pinned her under his big body again when he rolled them to the center of the bed.

A cry of protest sounded when he pulled his mouth away but he buried it against her throat to nip with his fangs. His hot lips kissed their way down to her breast to tease the taut nipple he scraped with his teeth. Her back arched off the mattress and her nails dug into his shoulders when he sucked hard.

"Fuck me."

He released her breast and jerked his head up. His sexy eyes appeared more feral, the color nearly black now, and his breathing increased. "Strip." He braced his arms, lifted and rolled off to give her room.

They both frantically wiggled out of their remaining clothes. Brand got naked first and flipped onto his back. His cock stood proudly, hard, and held her full attention. His fingers spread on his chest to skim over his nipples, his flat belly, all the way to his hips.

"Come here, hon."

She dropped on the bed to crawl up him with one of his legs between hers, and paused when her face hovered over the thick shaft of his cock. Her tongue darted out to wet her lips and Brand's gaze narrowed as his hands lifted to cup her face.

"I can't look at you enough, touch you enough, and it *still* feels like a dream."

"How about a wet one?"

She dropped her gaze to his lap and opened her mouth. The tip of her tongue swiped the crown of his shaft and swirled in a circle. His body jerked on the bed but he held still after that initial lack of control. A soft purr burst from her and her chest vibrated from the source.

Warmth seeped through her until her body felt as if it were on fire. It surprised her that she was reacting so intensely to Brand. He must have sensed how much she needed it, because he was going to allow her to taste him this time.

He was sexy as hell and she wanted him, but her level of need was off the charts of normal, under the circumstances. It wasn't her time to go into heat but there was no denying the symptoms. Her gums even ached a little as she wrapped her lips around him and sucked his cock deeper into her mouth.

"Fuck," he growled.

Don't grow fangs, she pleaded with her body. *If he realizes, he'll make me stop.* The tingling along the top row of her teeth persisted as she coaxed her mate into a fever of passion. The taste of his pre-cum on her tongue only seemed to draw forth her more basic instincts until she tore away from him, fearful of causing him harm. She felt her eyes changing as her vision became brighter and more vivid.

"Oh god," she panted. Her hand covered her mouth and the pain assured her that it wasn't her imagination. The sharp points pressed against her palm as her fangs elongated. She stared into Brand's dark eyes and knew he realized what was happening to her.

"Hon?" Alarm widened his eyes.

"Muh fangs." She winced, hearing the lisp.

His hands caged her ribs and rolled them. "Let me see."

Charma hesitated before sliding her hand away. Brand's gaze lowered to stare at her sharp teeth. His nostrils flared and he came down over her. One hand grabbed her knee to shove it up, giving freer access for his hips to sink into the cradle of her parted thighs.

She threw her head back as his thick cock drove into her. He captured her wrists and jerked them above her head, holding them there as he drove his cock deeper inside her body. She screamed as ecstasy hit so powerfully that she wasn't sure she could survive. Brand snarled as he nuzzled her hair to the side and his teeth bit into her shoulder.

He held her down as he fucked her frantically, bit deeper, and she wrapped her legs high around his waist. She couldn't move any other way as he furiously rode her. The heat level inside her body threatened to burn her alive as pleasure hammered her as hard as Brand did. His scent filled her nose, so sharp and wonderfully masculine. He was hers.

The need to taste him became overpowering. She lifted her head. She hadn't planned to bite him, but her sharp teeth sank into the top of his shoulder.

The taste of blood sent her into orgasm. Her body convulsed from the intensity of it and her mate seemed to be seized with ecstasy at the same time, as he snarled more savagely while his semen filled her.

They twitched, locked together, lost in passion. The sharp jolts of her climax slowly became weaker until she released him with her teeth and licked the wound she'd created. Reality returned. The mouth on her shoulder no longer bit but instead kissed.

"Fuck, hon," Brand groaned. "You're in heat."

She panted too hard to respond but nodded. There was no doubt about what had happened to her. It was the only time she grew fangs or claws. His hold on her wrists eased as he shifted enough to stop crushing her chest under his much bigger one. She breathed easier once she could completely fill her lungs. Brand raised his head and peered down at her.

"Sorry. I didn't want you to tear up my back."

"It's okay. I understood."

He searched her eyes. "You look stunned."

"I wasn't supposed to go into heat."

"It's not that time?"

She shook her head, still dazed. "No."

A smile played at his mouth. "Was I rough enough? I realized what was happening when I saw your fangs and remembered how you needed it fast and forceful. You used to swear that foreplay was sheer torture of the bad kind."

"That was amazing."

"Yeah. It was." He chuckled and slowly moved his hips, testing the feel of her pussy gripping his cock. "You're so damn hot and tight. I forgot how you swell a little and get so wet."

Charma moaned and it urged Brand to keep moving inside her. He adjusted again and his fingers laced through hers while his elbows held his upper body off her. She arched her back and lifted her legs higher, until her heels dug into his firm, muscular ass cheeks. She could feel them flex with every drive of his cock.

"More."

"You got it, hon." His mouth sought hers.

174

Their fangs brushed and she turned her head a little to avoid causing damage to either of them. His were extended, and she couldn't control hers for anything when she was in heat. Her shifter side kind of went crazy since it was the only time it was allowed out.

Every growl Brand made only excited her more. The vibrations in her chest returned when she began to purr. It was unsettling at first, trying to adjust to it, made breathing difficult, but she concentrated on how good it felt to have Brand fucking her.

Her vaginal walls clenched and she cried out when she came again. Brand spread his thighs a little and drove into her deeper, fighting to keep moving when she squeezed his cock tighter.

"Fuck," he rasped. "Oh yeah!"

His body tensed and he threw his head back. The howl he let loose startled Charma but she opened her eyes to watch his face as he found his own release again. His eyes closed, and the sheen of sweat on his big body and his nearly agonized expression were so sexy. Her gaze lowered to his broad shoulders and the fresh, still-bleeding bite wound she'd put on him. Her mark would leave a scar. A smile curved her lips as he stopped moving and tried to recover.

His still-black eyes opened as his chin lowered and their gazes held. "I love you."

"I love you too. This time I'm not sorry."

175

One of his eyebrows arched in question.

"For marking you."

He grinned. "Honey, you can bite me anytime." A chuckle escaped. "On my shoulder. You're not getting near my dick with those fangs. I'd be no good to either of us until I healed if you accidently bite me there."

"Too true."

"You had no idea you were going into heat? Did you stop keeping track of that stuff?"

"It wasn't supposed to happen. I think my emotions and being near you kind of sent me into it. I've heard of it happening when mates are separated for a long time, but only with long-term matings. It also might be your pheromones. You smell incredible when you're in heat."

"I always said you were my mate but we just hadn't cemented the deal by sharing bites during sex." His smile faded. "You felt the same way."

"I did," she admitted.

"I want to kill something when I think of all the years we lost."

Sadness gripped her hard and she squeezed his fingers, still laced with hers. "We've got a lot of years to look forward to."

"I'm never letting you go."

"Don't."

"I won't." He smiled. "When were you due to go into heat?"

176

Charma hesitated. "I don't. I mean, I haven't in a really long time."

Brand's smile faded as confusion set in. "I don't understand. Are you saying that you don't go into heat anymore, ever?"

"I really don't think you want to have this discussion right now."

"I do." He adjusted his body to keep her pinned. "I know you took pills to prevent the heat but you're far too young to have stopped naturally."

She was afraid to hurt him by mentioning Garrett. She gave him the short version, hoping it would be enough. "I had to keep taking the pills all the time and it seemed to send me into menopause."

"But you only ever took them when you started going into heat."

She hesitated but knew Brand wasn't going to let it go. "Let's skip this."

A muscle in his jaw jerked and his eyes narrowed. "Talk to me, damn it. Is this something to do with that asshole you were forced to be with?"

She nodded sharply. "I don't want to talk about him ever again."

"What are you not telling me? You said you'd never lie to me, hon."

"I don't want you to get angry."

"Tell me, because whatever I'll imagine has to be worse."

She studied his eyes. "I doubt it."

"Damn it, Charma. *Tell me.*"

It was a direct order from her mate. She knew the tone, although with Brand, it wasn't harsh or didn't imply he'd inflict pain if she disobeyed his demand. "I just didn't want to ruin the moment by answering. It doesn't matter anymore. I'm off the pills and obviously I can go into heat."

"You're stalling."

She took a deep breath and prepared for his rage. It wouldn't be directed at her, but she hated to expose him to all the horrors she'd been through. "Okay. I told you I took the pills to avoid going into heat and getting pregnant when I was with Garrett."

"Yeah." His fingers caressed hers.

"He got angry when I didn't go into heat. I never wanted to be with him. I couldn't stand him touching me and the thought of..." She closed her eyes. "You know how I get. I couldn't stomach knowing I'd..." She stopped talking, unable to say it to the man she loved.

"Shit." He sounded unhappy. "You'd have accepted him if you were in heat. Welcomed his touch."

She nodded.

"Look at me, hon."

Her eyes opened and she met his gaze.

"It's the bad part of being a shifter. When nature calls, she's one mean bitch in that regard."

Tears slipped out though she tried to hold them back. "I would have begged to be touched if the heat got hold of me, and I hated him. The thought of being that vulnerable and needy around him sickened me."

"Fuck." He was pissed but controlled his temper. "What did you do?"

"I took the pills, but then he got angry when I never went into heat and he injected me with drugs, trying to force it."

A snarl tore from Brand. "He drugged you to make you want him?"

"He threatened me with it first, so I was able to plan ahead and avoid him forcing me into heat. I took the pills every day, Brand. I never knew when he'd come after me with those injections. The pills counteracted the drugs as long as they were in my system. They weren't designed to be taken every day, the way I was popping them. After two years, I no longer even felt the heat coming on. There were no urges at all. They also suppressed my appetite, so I started losing weight. That was an added bonus, because I wasn't attractive to him anymore."

He lowered his head and brushed a kiss on her forehead. "I understand. I'm so sorry you had to do that."

"It's not your fault."

He pulled back and surprised her when he smiled. It reached his eyes. "I don't need to drug you to make you want me."

"No, you don't." She was relieved he wasn't punching walls or snarling. "I love *you*."

"I love you too, hon." His humor faded. "I'm still going to kill that son of a bitch the first chance I get."

"Okay. Just don't risk your life to take his. I couldn't stand to lose you."

"It's not ever happening. You're stuck with me." He winked.

She laughed. "Good."

"Speaking of us, do you want to go another round or do you want to eat first? I could fuck you all d—"

A knock sounded on the door.

"Go away!" Brand yelled.

"Um, you're needed downstairs," Braden called out. "I heard you two going at it. Don't I get points for waiting until you were done? Anton said to get you pronto. The pride has been spotted in town and they're headed this way."

"Fuck!"

Fear gripped Charma as she stared up into Brand's handsome face. He could get hurt. She could have found him again, only to lose him.

"Did you hear me? Are you coming? I mean, going downstairs? I know you just came. My ears are still ringing from that howl and I was two floors below, man."

"Go away, Braden. I'll be there soon."

"Okay."

His footsteps faded down the stairs. Brand gently tugged to get her to let go of his hands but she refused.

"I'm needed, Charma."

"Swear you'll come back to me."

"Nobody is going to stop me from returning to this bed really soon. I have too much to live for."

She let go but it was a tough thing to do.

He paused before he pulled away. "You stay up here. Lock the door and barricade it. I doubt they'll get inside the house but... There's a shotgun under the bed with a box of shells. Use it if you come under attack."

"I will."

He inhaled. "Don't worry. I'm not going to let anyone hurt you."

"The fear you smell isn't for me."

A smile softened his mouth. "I'm going to kick their asses. No worries."

She sat up to watch him dress. "Go for their faces."

He glanced at her before pulling his shirt over his head. "Why?"

"Pride males are very vain and conceited."

"Seriously?"

She hesitated. "Yes, they really care about their appearances. Sometimes it's the only thing they have going for them. You claw up their faces and they'll freak out."

"Scars are sexy." He winked.

"*I* think so, but they don't. Just be careful."

"I'll be back soon."

He left and she slid off the bed to rush toward the door. He waited on the other side until she locked it. A smile curved her lips. "I'll barricade it now. Go. Your family is expecting you."

A deep chuckle sounded through the door. "You're a great mate for taking orders."

"Don't get used to it."

He laughed as his footsteps receded down the stairwell. Charma turned and glanced around, spotting some old, heavy furniture in the shadows. She highly doubted any of the pride would breach the house filled with werewolves but she didn't want to take a chance of coming face-to-face with anyone from her old life. They'd kill her on sight if they discovered she'd warned the Harris Pack of their pending attack. She was a traitor to her own kind.

Her gaze slid to the bed. She should have told Brand she didn't know anything about weapons, but it was a comfort to know a shotgun was there.

* * * * *

Brand glanced around the basement at the pack males holding various conversations while they waited for everyone to arrive. Anton frowned at Rave for some reason, seeming upset. He walked over to the brothers.

"Is there a problem?" He kept his voice low to avoid being overheard.

"Yes," Anton hissed.

"No," Rave answered at the same time.

"Okay." Brand glanced between them. "What *isn't* the problem then?"

Rave crossed his arms over his chest. "Anton isn't happy that I brought a guest home."

"It's too dangerous." Anton glared at his brother.

"She's safer with me than on her own."

"Really? We're at war with a bunch of pissed-off cats. Explain to me why she wouldn't be better off far from here."

Rave hesitated. "It's complicated."

"I'm all ears."

"I'm just nosy," Brand whispered.

His cousins both shot him a grin and he was happy the tension eased between them. The last thing anyone in the pack needed was for the alpha's sons to show stress. There was enough of that going around already with the news of the approaching enemy.

Rave spoke. "She came to me for help. It's a long story but she wasn't safe with her pack. She was already in danger from *them*. She asked for asylum with our pack, and I gave it to her."

"Fine." Anton looked annoyed but he calmed down a bit. "We'll discuss this later. Did you get her settled in your old room?"

"Yeah. Sorry we were late."

Grady stepped into their tight huddle and smiled. "What are we whispering about?"

"Rave brought someone here that we don't know," Anton whispered.

"That's not all that strange. He's always bringing women home." Grady brushed his shoulder against the brother in question. "Is she hot?"

"Yeah." Rave grinned.

Grady shrugged. "Mystery solved. Are we ready?"

Anton glanced around the room. "Yes. I think everyone who was able to come is here." He turned, faced the room and moved to the center of it. One loud growl from him caused the room to go silent as all conversation ceased.

"The pride males were spotted in town and at the bar, where they asked for directions to this house." He paused. "We made sure no wolves were there, hoping to draw them in. They were given the information by the few humans we hired for that purpose. It was reported that the pride hasn't started any trouble yet. I'd guess they're going to attack really soon though."

"What humans?" Clover Arris frowned. "You told them what was going on?"

Rave answered. "No. They're some biker friends of mine who have no clue what I really am. They don't ask a lot of questions and some of them owed me a few favors, which I called in. I gave them orders to just direct anyone who came looking for a Harris to this house."

"What do they think is going on?" Brand was a little curious about the humans his cousin had planted at the family-run bar to feed information to the invading pride.

"I told them I'd gotten into debt gambling. As I said, my friends don't ask many questions."

"Aren't you afraid they'll get hurt?" Thomas Krid spoke.

"No." Rave chuckled. "These aren't your typical humans. They're good at lying and aren't easily intimidated. They'll also split right after their shift ends and leave town, no questions asked. We couldn't exactly have Yon bartending, or any of the other pack

185

members on staff there. The pride would have been on the attack, not just asking directions."

"What about the other humans in town? The pride could screw with our pack by causing trouble for them." Raymond Borl shook his head, a look of disgust plastered on his surly features. "They're lambs to the slaughter if we aren't around to protect them. We should go into town and attack the cats there."

"That's why you're not an alpha." Anton glared at him. "The last place we want this to go down is so close to innocent people. Some of their houses aren't far from the main strip, and they'd hear the fighting taking place in town."

"What about the ones who *do* know about us?" It was Timmy McQuire who asked.

"We told them trouble was coming and to go visit family. Hopefully they all got out."

"But what if these idiots still attack some of the humans?" Timmy questioned again.

"Prides are stricter about keeping secrets than we are," Rave answered. "It's a death sentence in most prides to reveal what they are to anyone who isn't a shifter."

"How do you know?" Raymond Borl asked.

Grady growled at him. "I've heard enough shit from you. What is *up* with you being the loudmouth of contention lately?"

Rave stepped closer. "I know because I've dealt with all kinds of shifters. Who do you think my father sends to talk to them when we've had boundary issues? Me."

The older man didn't look convinced. "We've never had anyone attack us before. This is what happens when you don't stick with your own kind."

Anton snarled.

Brand felt his own fangs growing longer. This conversation concerned Charma too. "Be very careful of what you say, Raymond. You might be the first to go if you want to start thinning the pack."

Braden stepped between them and the older man and faced him down. "I know you're old school, but you're being an idiot. Brand's way nicer than my brothers. Have you noticed how they aren't like Dad? Dad would have just smacked you down by now, but *they* will kill you. Now sit down and be smart. Shut up."

The older man didn't look happy but he sat. "I'm still worried about our human neighbors. They need us to protect them."

Rave looked ready to lunge at Raymond but it wasn't Brand who prevented bloodshed. Braden handled the situation.

"I know about prides too. They're totally anal about keeping shifter secrets. They make *us* look lax about that. Dad sent me to deal with a few of them when Rave was busy. They aren't about to do anything that will expose what they are to our human neighbors. We're the targets."

"When did Dad do that?" Rave touched Braden's shoulder to get his attention.

The youngest Harris shot him a quick look. "Someone likes to go to biker rallies sometimes. Life doesn't stop just because you leave town."

"Why you and not me?" Anton frowned. "I didn't know that either."

Braden grinned. "Dad knows I'm up for anything that involves pussies—and I'm good with them."

Grady smacked him on the back of the head. "Funny. Let's cut the shit and deal with this mess."

"Yeah," Brand agreed. He wanted to get this over with and return to Charma as soon as possible. He knew she had to be afraid in a house full of werewolves. He glanced upward, hoping she was okay.

Anton backed away from their small circle to address the room. "The prides are coming here and they want a fight." His eyes transformed to show his inner wolf while his fangs grew. "We're going to make them regret invading our territory."

"Hell yeah," Kane growled, rallying his enforcers. "We're more than up for it."

Brand laughed. "It was a bad decision to hit us during mating heat. You know our pack motto. If you can't fuck, fight!"

Braden chuckled. "I want a leather jacket with those words printed across my back."

Rave glared at him. "He was kidding."

"I'm not. We should make it our official slogan while Dad is allowing us to lead the pack."

Chapter Nine

Charma couldn't sit still after she'd barricaded the door. Worry for Brand and his pack left her feeling nervous and edgy. She turned off all the lights and opened the window. Fresh air breezed inside the room as she peered out into the night.

The moon gave off enough light for her enhanced vision to take in all the details of everything going on around the side of the house she viewed. Heavy woods surrounded the property but the trees had been cut back far enough to make it impossible for anyone to sneak close enough to break in. Sentries were posted, their dark shapes barely distinguishable unless someone was looking for them, as she was.

She eased down to her knees, rested her chin on her folded hands on the windowsill, and strained her ears for any noises beyond the branches whispering in the wind. It was only a matter of time before the attack began.

No way could she stand to lose Brand. *Life can't be that cruel, right?* She chewed on her bottom lip, hoping not. They'd both been through too much for fate to separate them once more.

Temptation pulled at her to use the cell phone Brand had forgotten when he'd left. She doubted anyone would try to retrieve her but she wasn't willing to chance it. Her car had been a piece of shit. No way would Garrett have spared the expense of putting any kind of system on it that could be tracked.

She crawled over and retrieved Brand's cell phone. It was a nice one and it took her a minute to figure out how to use it. She dialed Megan's cell, not wanting to deal with her parents. They'd be angry that she'd fled the pride and she wasn't sure she could trust them. It was sad but true. Both of them were grateful to the pride for being alive.

It rang twice before her sister picked up. "Who is this?" Alarm was clear in her voice. "How did you get this number?"

"Hi, Meg. It's Charma."

"Who is B. Harris? Where are you? Garrett called and came over here looking for you. He seemed worried."

She refrained from snorting. He was such a good liar. "I left him. I'm not coming back."

Silence ensued and she imagined her sister was a little shocked. "He beat you again, didn't he?"

It was Charma's turn to be a little stunned. Did her whole family know?

"Char?" Meg lowered her voice and a door closed. "Are you hurt? Do you need me to come to you? Some of the pride are nearby but I can sneak out. Tell me what you need and where you are. I know Darbin and my mate can't protect you without starting a war between our prides, but we can help. Do you need money? Where did you go? Are you safe?"

"You knew Garrett hit me sometimes?"

A small sniff escaped Megan. "I suspected but had no proof. I do now. I never saw your mate treat you as well as Cole does me. I'm so sorry. You did it to protect us, didn't you? I wondered why you mated Garrett. You always said he was a prick but then you agreed to be with him after you returned from college. You've always refused to answer my questions but Cole and I talked. He said you might have done it for us, the family."

"Yeah." Charma sat on the floor, leaned against the bed. "Percy is a bastard. You know how he rules. He wanted me mated to his son and that was the end of it."

"Darbin isn't anything like him. My father-by-mate is pretty awesome."

"I'm glad you ended up with a good pride, honey. I called to tell you that I'm safe."

"Have you called our parents?"

"No."

"Are you going to?"

"No. You can't tell them about the name on the caller ID. I'm trusting you, Meg. I doubt Garrett will come after me but I'm not willing to risk it. Okay?"

"Is this B. Harris a friend of yours?"

192

She hesitated. "It's a long story."

"I have all the time in the world for you."

She hesitated but knew she could trust her sister. "I met him in college and we fell in love. I had to give him up for the family. I ran to him, and that's who I'm with. I'm safe and he still loves me."

Her sister sucked in air. "A human?" She recovered before Charma could speak. "Okay. I can deal with that. You can hide what you are from him, and hell, I guess you could get him drunk when you go into heat and feed him Viagra to help him keep up with your sex drive. He'll just think he became some mega stud. I won't judge."

"Um..."

"No. It's okay," Meg insisted. "Since you don't shift, you can pull it off. Just dye your hair...tell him those spots down your back are faded tattoos you got while you were drunk as a teen. Contacts can be worn for days at a time. You can take them out while he's not with you. Does he live near pride lands? Are you close to us? Because Darbin can order our people to never mention it if they see you. Just be real careful."

"He's not human."

"Oh my god. You ran off with a pride male? I don't remember a Harris as one of Percy's. Is he one of Darbin's? I haven't met the ones who live farther out." Her voice lowered to a murmur. "Are you in our pride? Shit! It's okay though. Darbin can order them not to mention you're here. That will probably work out better."

"Brand isn't a pride member," she admitted. "He's a werewolf."

"*What?*" her sister shouted.

Charma winced. "Calm down."

Her sister lowered her voice to a whisper. "A werewolf? Is that what you said?"

"Yes. We met at college and lived together."

Total silence.

"Are you still there, Meg?"

"I am." Her sister took a ragged breath. "I'm flabbergasted."

"I know."

"He doesn't try to eat you?"

Charma couldn't help but laugh. "Every chance he gets, but in a good way."

"Oh!" Meg laughed too. "Got it." She sobered. "Is he good to you?"

"We love each other, and he is amazing. I mated him."

Her sister gasped.

"I know what you're thinking."

"You're already mated."

"Was. Not anymore, not to Garrett. Brand is my true mate."

"This is a lot to take in."

"I know. I don't want you to worry. You can tell the family I'm safe but nothing else."

"Mom and Dad would flip if they knew any of this. They'd tell Garrett and Percy. You can't trust them."

"I know."

"I'll keep your secret. You saved our lives. Cole and I suspected you prevented us from being turned into breeders. That was it, wasn't it?"

There was no reason to lie. "Yeah. Percy threatened to kill our parents, along with Adam, and sell us off to other prides."

"What a fuckhead," Meg hissed. "I always hated him. He tried to prevent me from mating Cole. He wanted me to stay in his pride instead."

"I'm so sorry I couldn't give you any warning that I was leaving but I didn't have time."

"The important thing is you're safe and I know that." Megan paused. "I'm going to memorize this number and then delete it. I'll buy a disposable phone to call you and give you the new number. I don't want to risk Garrett hunting for you and trying to get hold of my phone to do it. I refuse to lose contact with you. Promise me that you'll stay in touch."

"I promise."

"A werewolf." Her sister chuckled. "You always were one to buck tradition. First it was college and now this."

"He's amazing, Megan. I wish you could meet him."

"I plan to see you. Once Cole gets home from his trip, we'll figure it out."

Charma's breath froze in her lungs. "What trip?"

"The Prides called a joining and he's been sent to help fight our enemy."

"Oh shit. Can you call him?"

"Yes. He always keeps his cell with him."

"Tell him and the others of your pride to come home *right now*. Save his life."

"Why?" Megan sounded alarmed.

"It's *my* pack, Megan. My mate's, anyway. That's who the council plans to attack. The werewolves aren't plotting to eradicate our kind. A neighboring pride came into their territory and kidnapped a she-cat mated to a werewolf. They had to kill to get her back."

"Fuck." Megan panted.

"Yeah. Call your mate, but you can't tell him I'm here or why he can't allow your pride to fight with the werewolves. Whoever is with him might overhear the conversation."

"What a nightmare."

Charma couldn't agree more.

"I'll tell him I smelled werewolf in the woods behind our house. His duty to protect us overrides everything else. It will send them rushing back here."

"You'd lie for me?"

"In a heartbeat. I'll tell him the truth once he's home. He'll understand. Plus, talk about making bad first impressions upon meeting your family-by-mate. A battleground isn't ideal, and no damn way are we going to allow our mates to kill each other. I love you. I'll call you in a few days—or call me if things go bad there."

"I love you too. Call your mate now."

"I'm on it."

Charma replaced Brand's cell phone where he'd left it and hugged her chest. She should have thought about the fact that Darbin might be asked to send some of his males to fight, probably his own son, but she hadn't considered much beyond reaching Brand's pack to warn them so he'd be safe. She knew Megan would talk Cole into coming home with their males. The werewolves would have fewer pride to fight.

She crawled back across the floor to the window, staying low in case any of the pride males were in the woods and had climbed trees to get a look inside the windows.

She peeked outside, searching the night with her enhanced vision. She closed the window to mask her scent. It would be stronger while she was in heat.

* * * * *

Brand pressed tightly against the trunk of the tree he'd climbed. The pride wouldn't expect wolves to attack from above. He glanced across the open area to seek out the other members of his pack, hiding in similar locations surrounding the house. The scent of their enemy hadn't reached them yet but reports had come in that out-of-town cars had parked along the road leading into the woods.

A slight noise drew his attention. He turned his head and saw a dark figure creeping out of the basement door. His hands clenched in anger as he watched Braden dart away. His cousin had been ordered to stay inside but he'd obviously disobeyed Anton. He almost called out, to demand he get his ass back inside, but reconsidered, not willing to give away his location in case the pride had approached without detection. It was possible.

His cousins were going to wring their youngest brother's neck when they realized he'd joined the fight. Part of Brand sympathized with Braden. He knew all about being young and making bad choices. Charma talking him out of mating her when he'd been lucky enough to find the right woman had been the worst one. He'd come home angry and bitter. He'd been lonely without her and used violence as an outlet. Braden might be experiencing the same affliction, since he was horny as hell and banned from fucking anyone in the pack. The heat made it ten times worse.

The wind shifted and the faint stench of cat teased his nose. He jerked his head in that direction and reached for the infrared binoculars hanging around his neck. His eyesight was excellent but they helped him see farther. He caught a slight movement and zoomed in.

A group of seven strangers were by the creek, about to climb up the embankment on the north side. He started to signal his pack but something odd happened.

A tall man withdrew something from his pocket that he guessed was a phone. He seemed to listen for long seconds and then a quick hand motion had all of them turning and rushing away in the opposite direction.

It worried Brand. They either had fled in fear from the coming fight or they had a new target. Braden hadn't gone in that direction so he knew they weren't pursuing his cousin. He used the binoculars to track the strangers through the trees. They were moving fast, running at full speed, heading directly toward the old cemetery. No pack homes were in that area but there was a road.

He climbed higher when the tops of other trees blocked his view and finally spotted the dark line of pavement. No street lights had been placed that far out but lights came on. They were faint. He watched as two sets of twin beams picked up speed, curving out of sight.

They were leaving. The road they traveled would take them away from the pack.

Brand climbed down to his original spot on the thick branch, pondering why the seven pride members had fled. Had they scented all the wolves lying in wait and decided it wasn't a good night to die?

A smile curved his lips. They might not have a fight after all. The pride seemed to be on the run. His lips parted to speak, his intention to tell the others, but an owl hoot silenced him. He craned his neck to search for the source, finding Rave in another tree a few dozen yards away.

His cousin pointed and he caught a glimpse of movement. He lifted his binoculars again and located nearly a dozen more strangers. They cautiously used the foliage to advance. The wind blew in the wrong direction to pick up their scent but it was obvious they weren't friendly.

He removed the binoculars and hooked the strap on the tree, staring at Anton. His cousin glanced around, seeming to wait until he had everyone's attention. A few quick hand motions signaled their orders.

Brand removed his shirt but kept the sweatpants on since they wouldn't hinder movement. His shoes had been left inside the house. He bent and crawled farther out on the thick branch until he lay flat on his stomach. It wasn't the most comfortable position he'd ever been in but it was necessary. It was an easy eight-foot drop to the ground. It was just a matter of waiting for the enemy to draw closer.

He kept still, his rage building. The alpha blood would allow him to shift completely within seconds of his feet hitting the ground. His fingertips tingled as his nails grew into sharp claws and hair sprouted along his skin to protect it against the rough bark of the tree. He and his cousins would attack first, to give the other enforcers at least thirty seconds to complete their transformations into full wolves.

The pride inched closer, seemingly oblivious to the danger above them. Brand glanced toward the alpha house, his gaze on the uppermost window, near the roofline. Charma had closed the window and it was dark up there, but he could sense her watching, waiting for him to return. His determination to kill the invaders and end the war as quickly as possible made him impatient.

The pride came forward, using bushes and trees in an attempt to hide their approach. He watched as a few of them took to the trees.

A smile curved his lips when the first pride male came into contact with Rave. A howl ripped the silence as two large figures crashed to the ground in a jumble of fighting limbs. Brand dropped to the ground and attacked a pride member who rushed to assist the one getting thrashed by his cousin. The male hissed before his fingers sprouted sharp claws. Brand snarled, showing his fangs, and tore into the man's upper shoulder as they clashed.

He ignored the sounds of fighting as his pack engaged the pride members. A lot of pent-up anger surged out of him. He just wished he could take out his rage on the one who'd mated and abused Charma. She'd said the son of a bitch hadn't been sent to wage war, just amplifying his belief that the guy was a pussy in every sense of the word. The day would come, though, he silently swore, that he'd track that animal down.

"Keep a few alive," Anton snarled, loud enough to be heard.

It didn't make sense to Brand but he followed orders, just severely maiming his opponent. The shifter stopped fighting once Brand used his claws to slash the male's right cheek open and then broke his shoulder. He left him huddled in pain and attacked another leopard streaking toward the house.

The thing was fast, but Brand caught him by his back leg mid-leap when he attempted to jump onto the second floor landing. His teeth sank into the leopard's meaty thigh. The male yowled in pain and crashed to the ground. He rolled over, his claws slicing at the thick fur protecting Brand's chest, but Brand rolled to the side, avoiding the deadly strike as the shifter went for his heart. He inwardly winced at the thought of the new scars he'd have.

They both slammed through the living room windows, into the house.

More werewolves attacked the male as Brand backed away, leaving the poor bastard to his fate. The cat only made it a few feet inside before he was dead. Brand jumped back outside and scanned the yard for other threats to the house.

He figured they were searching for Alpha Elroy, to kill him. They wouldn't find his uncle, since he was miles away, hidden, locked inside the pack doctor's basement. Another leopard caught his attention. That one was using the treetops to launch an attack on the house. He landed on the roof and Brand howled a warning to the ones inside. He turned, barreled back through the broken windows and jumped over the carcass of his enemy.

His bulkier, hairy body filled the stairwell and his claws tore into the carpet. He didn't give a damn because that leopard was too close to Charma.

It was tough to distinguish noises, with all the battles taking place, but he heard glass break and a female scream.

Charma! No!

He went insane as he bolted to the second floor and crashed through a window at the end of the hallway. He almost skidded off the narrow roof but his claws tore into the wood shingles, holding his ground as he started to climb toward the third floor. He'd ordered her to barricade the door and knew it would be faster to reach her from the windows. Werewolves weren't designed to climb but he was motivated. He slid on the steep incline.

Brand howled in rage and had to take a few calming breathes. He forced his wolf back enough to lose his claws and regain his hands. He tried to climb but slid farther. He turned his head and jumped toward the tree that the leopard had used to reach the third floor. He couldn't climb as a wolf but he could as a man. It was slow going but he had to reach Charma.

It was eerily silent above as he finally reached the branch that was close enough for him to peer in through the windows that had been breached. He stared inside — and what he saw made him want to roar in outrage.

Charma cowered beside a dresser that had been pulled into one corner of the room. A leopard had her trapped there, blocking her escape.

The pride male stood just feet from where she huddled. That male could be Garrett.

Rage gripped Brand as he recovered enough to catch his breath and inch along the branch toward the opening. He was going to kill that son of a bitch for getting too close to his mate.

Chapter Ten

The big beast crashed through the windows. Charma gasped and rolled out of the way when the leopard paused to shake off the broken glass. Terrified by his violent entry, she managed to stumble to her feet but there was no escape. She wedged into the corner beside the dresser she'd used to block the door. The shotgun was behind the intruder, out of her reach.

The male shook his furry body again, removing the last of the debris, and straightened. His head swung her way and she identified his features and eyes. She'd spent way too much time with Percy and the enforcers not to know what they looked like shifted as well as in skin. Surprise widened his eyes when his gaze landed on her and his vision adjusted to the dim room.

Oh shit. He's going to kill me. She had no doubt about that. The last time she'd seen Randy in Percy's office, he'd been considering mounting her until the pride leader had forbidden him to take her.

Time seemed to freeze. She didn't glance away from him until he moved a step in her direction.

She grabbed at the only thing within reach. A vase on top of the dresser. She grasped the base and smashed off the top. "Stay back!"

He began to shift and she saw his nose flare as he sniffed. He'd picked up her change in scent. Brand's mark would offend him—

and he'd also know she'd gone into heat. Her fangs elongated but she kept her lips closed, hoping he didn't notice her fingernails were clawed as well. She needed any advantage she could get to survive.

Brand, where are you? She silently screamed for him but knew her mate was probably fighting for his own life.

Randy's voice came out a mix of pissed-off man and outraged leopard. "What are you doing here?"

"I came to warn them." She braced her back against the wall and inched her other hand behind the edge of the dresser. He'd have to come at her, and she planned to push the dresser in the way when he did.

"You *what*?" He took a threatening step forward but stopped, his mouth hanging open.

"I warned them," she taunted, praying she'd be able to send him into a rage. He wouldn't be thinking, would be more focused on just tearing her apart, and that was the only advantage she had. "I told them the pride called a joining."

"Why would you betray us that way?"

"Why do you think?" She finally lifted her chin, allowing him to see her fangs. "I loathe the pride."

He didn't strike out at her the way she figured he would. He took a step back, his face paling. "You stink of wolf!"

"I mated one."

206

His utter shock was apparent.

Attack now, her inner voice urged. She just wasn't brave enough to leave the tight space. Her instincts were playing hell and the shifter side of her wanted to hide from the larger, dangerous male threatening her. He was stronger, faster, and she wasn't about to fool herself that her odds of winning weren't slim to none. Her human half wanted to cause him some pain before he killed her.

"I have your sister," he finally spat.

It was her turn to be shocked. "What?"

"Breeanna followed us here, thinking we were tracking you." His eyes narrowed. "Put down the vase and follow me out of here, or I'll kill her."

"You're lying."

"I hate Percy too." He cocked his head, staring at her. "He wouldn't even send Garrett to fight for this cause. I'm sick of being fodder. With you and your sister, we could breed a new pride. You come with me without putting up a fight, and I won't kill her. I always wanted you," he hissed. "But first we'll have to rid you of that dog stench."

"You don't have Bree." She refused to believe him.

"I do." The smug expression on his face terrified her that he was telling the truth. "She's with my brother. He can have her, and I'll get you. I don't think you're defective." His gaze lowered down her body with interest. "I just think Garrett is as spineless as his father and shooting blanks. I know about him screwing anything that says yes, and none of them have ended up pregnant. Your mother was a breeder; she gave your father four kittens before the accident. I wanted you, but Percy said his precious boy could have you instead. Leave with me now or Breeanna will pay, Charma. I'm taking you with me either way, but I'll hurt *her* as your punishment if you put up a fight."

Her hold on the vase loosened. Randy took advantage of that by moving faster than she could react and grabbing hold of her wrist, violently snagging it with enough force to shake the broken object from her fingers. It crashed to the carpet and he yanked her out of her hiding spot.

He turned, prepared to drag her out the way he'd come, but the sight of Brand climbing through the window stopped them both.

Charma was never so happy to see her furious mate than at that moment, since she was too worried about her sister's fate to know what to do. He snarled and lunged forward.

Something wet splattered across her face and she turned her head, saw claws rip into Randy's chest, all the way through to his back.

He screamed and his hold on her was gone as Brand threw him across the room. Brand's elbow caught her shoulder, sending her crashing toward the bed. She landed facedown on the mattress, bounced once and realized what had happened. She twisted her head and watched Brand tear Randy apart. The gory sight was horrific. The pride enforcer never even got the chance to scream again before he died.

Brand turned, half man and half beast, panting. Fresh blood covered his skin and dripped off his claws. His eyes were all wolf as he stared at her.

Charma blinked a few times, in shock.

"Are you okay? I thought that might be Garrett but I can tell by his smell that he's not."

She had to adjust to his rough voice to understand what he said. She managed a nod. "He was an enforcer from my pride."

He took a step forward, then another, and dropped to his knees next to the bed. He kept his arms outstretched at his sides, his claws extended but far away from her.

"Charma, did he hurt you?" His voice was less growl now, more human.

She rolled over and sat up. "I'm okay. He said he has my baby sister." She turned her head to stare at what was left of Randy. Bile rose in her throat and she swallowed hard, avoiding the sight as she turned back to hold Brand's gaze.

"I'm sorry, baby." He inched closer but didn't touch her. "I thought you'd be safe up here."

"I'm okay. What if he really has my sister? He said Breeanna followed him here, and his brother has her."

209

Brand breathed hard but his claws slid back into his fingertips. He grabbed some of the bedding and wiped his hands on it. "Do you think he was telling the truth?"

"Yes. Maybe. I don't know. Bree can be pretty impulsive, so it's possible."

Brand slowed his breathing, reaching for control, and glanced around. He stared at something on the nightstand. "Does she have a phone? Call her."

Charma was still stunned but she nodded. Her sister had a habit of making rash decisions. Would she follow the males out of pride lands if she thought they were going after Charma? She crawled across the bed and snagged the phone. Her hands shook as she dialed her sister's number. It rang six times before going to voice mail.

"She's not answering. She always picks up."

"Maybe it's because she doesn't know the incoming number."

"That wouldn't stop her. She's close to a lot of humans and they're always changing their numbers." She waited for the beep. "Bree, this is Charma. This is urgent. You call me right back. Do you understand? At this number. Call me right now." She hung up.

Brand went to the cramped bathroom located in the corner of the room. The sound of running water made it clear he was washing away the blood. She clutched his cell phone, waiting for it to ring.

Every second seemed like a minute. A wet hand clamping down on her shoulder made her jump and stare up at Brand fearfully.

"She isn't calling back. What if she followed them?" Her gaze drifted to the broken windows facing the woods. "It's a war zone out there and my baby sister could be in the middle of it."

"We'll find her."

"Your pack would kill her, wouldn't they?" She panicked. "They'll think she's attacking them with the pride males."

Brand jerked her to her feet. "Let's take you downstairs to a safer location and I'll go look for her."

"How will you know who she is? You've never met her."

"She's a she-cat in pack territory. It won't be hard."

She clutched at him with her free hand, keeping hold of the phone with the other. "I need to go with you. She'll be terrified."

"Charma," Brand growled, "calm down, baby. Trust me. I need to get you downstairs to Kane and his brother. They can protect you. I'll go search for your sister. We aren't even sure if she's out there."

She wanted to go with him but knew she'd only slow him down. She tried to think rationally. "You can't go out there alone. Randy said his brother has Bree. There could be more than one enforcer with her. You'd be outnumbered."

"I can handle a few pussies."

It was a hellish situation for Charma. Brand could be in danger if he went to locate Bree. She was torn between the love for her baby sister and for her mate. Brand leaned in and pressed his forehead against hers.

"Trust me, hon. I'm going to find your sister if she's here. I know what direction they came from. I'll backtrack their footprints, okay?"

"Be careful. I can't lose you."

"Nothing is going to keep me from spending a long life with you," he swore. "Now come with me downstairs. Kane and Klax can guard you. Maybe I'll take Braden with me. He'll want to fight. Will that make you feel better?"

"Yes."

He released her and glanced once at the dead body of Randy. He cleared the door and turned, holding out a hand to her. "Come on, Charma. Time isn't on our side. The pride must be on the run by now. They aren't winning this war."

They hurried downstairs. The sounds of fighting inside the house could be heard and Charma saw a body on the floor when they reached ground level. Two tall blonds stood next to the bloodied corpse of a leopard. Both turned, growling at their approach. They saw Brand and lowered their clawed hands.

"Guard my mate," Brand ordered harshly. He released Charma. "Stay with them. They'll keep you safe."

"Where is Braden?" She frantically looked around.

"I'll find him." Brand rushed away.

Charma stared up at the identical twins with a bit of trepidation. They were big werewolves, something she'd always feared, but Brand said she'd be safe with them. She just didn't feel it as they regarded her with identical intense stares.

"Hi." She felt the need to say something, anything, to break the tension.

One of them turned away, sniffing. "More approach."

His brother moved fast, making Charma gasp when he just hooked her around her waist and swung her off her feet. She tried not to cringe, knowing that the wetness seeping through her clothes was blood from his fresh kill. She had other things to worry about. In four long strides, he took her to a door and yanked it open. "Be quiet," he ordered, dropping her on her feet. "Stay put. We won't let anyone reach you."

She was shoved inside a closet and the door closed, leaving her in darkness.

The phone in her hand rang and she startled then frantically accepted the call, hoping it was Bree.

"Hello?"

"I'm sorry," a female crooned. "I must have called the wrong number. I was trying to reach my ex-boyfriend."

213

"It's a new number I just got. Whoever you're trying to reach obviously changed theirs. Sorry," Charma whispered, hanging up. She didn't have time to deal with another Peggy situation.

She heard snarls and a battle taking place on the other side of the door. She leaned against the thick wood, hoping the two brothers were as fierce as they appeared. The prides seemed focused on attacking the alpha house. She closed her eyes and prayed Brand would be safe.

Brand rushed outside and headed in the opposite direction that Braden had gone, feeling a little guilt about lying to his mate. She'd worry less if she thought he had backup. He was torn between staying to protect Charma and going after her sister. The pride male could have lied in an attempt to get her to leave with him but he had to be certain.

He caught a leopard attempting to sneak up on the house and attacked. He wasn't in the mood to dally so he shifted fast and just tore into the male. He quickly left him dead on the lawn and sprinted in the direction the group of pride had come from. He had a good idea where they'd entered the woods. A lone stretch of road near the old graveyard would have allowed them the closest access to the alpha house.

His paws dug into the ground as he rushed forward, on alert for the enemy. He passed a few groups of wolves and four of them followed him, perhaps hoping he was on the scent of a new target.

214

He ignored the males, ones he didn't know. They were probably visitors for mating heat and had ignored orders to leave. He picked up a scent a few miles away and changed direction. Fresh blood from a kill alarmed him and he hoped it wasn't a female she-cat he'd find.

When he located the fallen body, it was a male who was in skin but stank of pride. A wolf had ripped open his chest. He leaned in, pressing his nose close. Another scent came through and he growled. Braden had taken out the male.

It became clear that Braden might have headed away from the fighting but he'd doubled back. Another snarl drew his attention and he turned his head, watching one of the strangers sniff the nearby grass.

He stepped over the body and shoved the male aside, sniffing at the spot. Female she-cat was distinctive.

The males let out a howl of intent to track her but he barreled into the one who seemed to be in charge, taking him to the ground. His teeth locked around the male's throat in warning.

NO! His wolf sent that signal out loud and clear. He released the male and threw his head in the direction of the alpha house. *Go!* His wolf snarled to emphasize the order.

The males whined in protest but obeyed. They turned tail and rushed in the opposite direction, leaving him at the scene alone. He waited, lowered his nose and investigated the faint scent of the she-cat. Braden's scent was there too.

Part of him was relived. Braden had found her, and Brand didn't find any traces of her blood. He discovered where her scent ended and studied the tracks. A pair of bare footprints a few feet away told him, from their deep imprint, that his cousin must have carried Charma's sister. He'd left in skin, as a man.

Braden had killed the male and taken the she-cat. It had to be Charma's sister, even though her scent didn't remind him of his mate's. His gaze landed on the torn-apart male lying in the woods. Braden could be immature at times but he wasn't one to lose his temper without cause. His cousin wouldn't harm a she-cat, especially one he'd killed for. Braden had killed the male while protecting her. The single set of footprints leading away indicated his cousin was taking her to town, away from the fighting.

Brand made a decision. He turned away from the tracks and plowed through the woods, back toward the alpha house. Charma was his priority. Howls ahead spurred him to run faster, wondering what they meant. He came across the she-cat's scent on his way to the house and paused; his jaw closed over her discarded jacket and he took it with him.

He rushed into the front yard of the alpha house and saw a lot of the enforcers celebrating. The fight was over. Dead bodies littered the ground but most of them were pride. He spotted a familiar wolf, down and motionless. Greif rose for a brief second when he realized

216

one of their enforcers had been lost. He shifted to skin, dropped the she-cat's coat on the ground and walked inside the house.

Kane and Klax grinned at him. Blood coated their bodies but they had kept their clothes on, not fully shifting into wolves. Charma wasn't with them and he was instantly concerned.

"Where's my mate?"

Klax winked. "In the closet, safe as can be." He pointed.

Brand yanked open the door and Charma nearly fell into his arms. She turned, staring up at him with wide eyes. He hugged her hard, hating the smell of fear rolling off her. Then another, scarier scent hit.

"I smell blood." He jerked away, staring at her waist.

"It's not mine."

His relief was instant. "Your sister is safe. At least a female she-cat is."

She clung to him. "Where is she?"

"Braden has her."

She wiggled in his arms, trying to look around him. "Where is Bree?"

"Braden took her to town, away from the fighting."

"Did she say her name was Bree? She's got long dark hair and big blue eyes. We kind of look alike too."

"I never saw her."

"What do you mean?" Her voice grew panicked. "You were with him, and you said he has her."

"Calm down," he urged. "Braden found her first and he killed the male who was with her."

She gasped.

"He wouldn't hurt her."

"How can you be sure?"

"She's a pussy." Klax snorted. "Killing is the last thing that pup would do to her."

"What does that mean?" Charma glared at the enforcer.

Brand instructed Kane to retrieve the jacket he'd left in the yard.

Kane went outside and brought the jacket, sniffing it. "She-cat. Does this smell like your sister?"

Charma broke free of his arms and lunged, snatching the jacket out of the enforcer's hand. She sniffed it and turned back to Brand. Tears filled her eyes as she clutched it against her chest. "I bought this for Breeanna." She reached inside one of the pockets and withdrew a cell phone. She showed it to him. "This is hers."

"Braden definitely has your sister then." He tried to pull her back into his arms, needing assurance that she was really okay after all the aggression of fighting. She resisted, staring up at him with the beginnings of anger stamping her pretty features.

"Let's go find her. I need to make sure she's fine."

218

Kane cleared his throat. "Um, if Braden has her, you might want to wait a few hours."

Brand grimaced and shot the blond a dirty look to shut him up. Charma gaped at Kane and then spun, facing Brand. "Why? What will Braden do?"

He grabbed her waist, tugging her closer. "He won't hurt her."

"He'll fuck her," Klax muttered.

Charma stiffened in his arms. "No!"

"I'm sure he won't," Brand lied, hoping his cousin wouldn't try to seduce his mate's sister. He didn't really believe that though. Braden was a horn dog. If Breeanna looked similar to Charma, his cousin would be attracted to her.

"We have to find them now!" Charma released the jacket with one hand and snagged his arm. "She's a virgin."

"Oh lord," Klax chuckled. "Not for long."

"Damn it," Brand growled, glaring at the twins. "This isn't amusing."

"It depends." Kane laughed. "It's not *my* mate's innocent sister who's with Braden so it is kind of funny."

"It is," Klax agreed.

Charma growled. "Brand, take me to them now. He can't touch her. She hasn't even had her coming-out party yet. She's got to be terrified of a werewolf."

"How old is she again?" Brand was afraid to hear the answer.

219

"Eighteen. She just graduated from high school."

"Old enough," Kane announced.

"Damn it, you're not helping!" Brand wanted to punch him.

"Brand!" Charma demanded his full attention. "Let's go."

"Not yet." Klax shook his head. "There are pride still out there fleeing. It's not safe."

"What if they run right to where my sister and your cousin are staying? They could be in trouble." Charma sounded frantic.

"He was taking her into town. That's the last place the pride wants to go. They're injured and some of them are too hurt to shift back into skin. They'll want to avoid humans." Kane was the voice of reason. "Braden is a lot of things but he's pussy friendly." He didn't bother to hide his smile. "No male is getting near your sister. He won't allow it while he's in heat."

Anton strode into the house butt naked and Brand winced when Charma gaped at his cousin before turning her head away from the sight of so much skin. She buried her face against his chest.

"We kept four of them alive," his cousin announced as he tore a curtain off the rod and wrapped it around his waist. "We're going to send a message back to those prides through them. Rave is handling that and escorting them back to their vehicles with some of our wolves, to make sure they survive that long."

"He's decent," Brand whispered to Charma, hooking an arm around her waist to keep her close as more wolves returned to the

220

house in different states of undress. Some had put on pants while others just strode in naked, looking for something to wear after shifting back to skin. "But you might want to keep your eyes up for a few minutes. We keep spare clothing in the basement," he said louder, letting everyone know.

Charma squeezed his arm. "My sister."

Anton frowned. "What about your sister?"

"She's in our territory," Kane stated. "Braden has her."

Anton groaned, shooting a dark look at Brand. "Why?"

"It's a long story."

"Make it a quick one," Anton demanded.

"She came with the pride males," Charma told him.

"To attack us?" Anton frowned.

"No!" She shook her head. "Breeanna isn't a fighter."

"She's a lover," Klax chuckled. "Or she will be if Braden has a say in the matter."

"Shit. You trusted my baby brother with your sister?" Anton scowled.

"*No.*" Charma pressed tightly against Brand.

"Charma's sister ended up in our territory after following some of the pride here. She thought they were coming after Charma. I tracked her down but Braden found her first. He carried her off

221

toward town. I returned here," Brand explained. "Charma wants to go find her sister but I keep telling her that Braden won't hurt her."

"He won't," Anton confirmed. "He's cat-friendly."

Klax laughed.

Anton and Brand both shot him silencing glares. He turned away. "I'll go assess the mess and start a bonfire to be rid of the bodies. We need to clear away any evidence of what happened here, before dawn. Von just returned and offered to handle that but he could use some help."

"Go help him, Kane," Anton ordered.

"What did I do?" The enforcer grinned though. "I'm going."

"My sister," Charma pressed.

Anton sighed. "She isn't in any danger if Braden has her. Right now we need to focus on the injured and make sure no stragglers are waiting around to attack us when our defenses are down." His tone deepened, befitting that of an alpha. "Brand, you and your mate can man the house. The enforcers can do most of the cleanup. I'm going to have to make calls to check on the pack and do a head count, to see who we've lost."

Brand nodded. He knew Charma wanted to argue but she kept quiet, tense in his hold. Anton left the house, issuing orders to the pack. She turned in his arms, staring up at him.

"I know," he whispered. "But right now we have to deal with the aftermath of this fight. Humans can't find out about us. That's

222

priority. There are dead bodies on the lawn and in the woods that they could stumble across. I'll call Braden. He probably took her to my house. It wasn't too far from where he found her."

Her shoulders squared. "Please call."

He released her and strode over to the nearest house phone and dialed his cousin's cell. It rang three times before going to voice mail. He clenched his teeth, waiting for the beep. "Braden, don't you touch that she-cat." He noticed Charma had followed him, so he watched what he said. "She's my mate's sister. Keep her safe and your pants on. Do you get my meaning? Call me back at the alpha house immediately. Charma is worried sick about Bree."

He hung up and turned. "He'll keep her safe. I know he won't hurt her."

"Why didn't he answer his phone? Maybe they need help."

"He rarely answers his phone. It's normal for him to keep the ringer off but he checks his messages often. He'll call back." He hoped that was true.

She didn't seem appeased.

"The pride doesn't have her, which is a good thing, right? You met Braden and you know he isn't prejudiced. He'll see her as a woman, not the enemy." He figured that was the main reason for her fear. "I'm sure she told him who she is because he'd have wanted to know why she entered our territory. He killed someone from your pride to protect her and get her away from him. I'm sure they're okay, probably locked inside my basement, waiting for the danger to pass. The best thing we can do is end this nightmare quickly so we can go home."

"You're right. Okay. What can I do to help? This is my pack now too."

He didn't want her dealing with any grisly tasks. "Food." He led her into the kitchen. "We're always hungry after shifting. Make as many sandwiches as possible." He caught the attention of one of the pack, motioning him over. "This is Dan. He's going to help you." He shot the male a menacing look. "This is my mate. You don't let her out of your sight. Protect her if there are any unfriendly faces coming in here looking for a meal. You help her feed them."

The younger male nodded but sniffed at her, his face showing surprise that she wasn't a wolf. "Okay."

"You have a problem with that?" Brand growled.

The pup shook his head. "No."

"Good." He took the jacket from Charma's arms and placed it on the back of a chair. "Your sister will be safe with my cousin. Don't worry about her right now, okay?"

She blew out a breath. "I don't have a choice, do I? If he touches her though…"

"He's not a rapist," Brand swore, certain Braden wouldn't force a woman no matter how bad the heat got. "You met him. He's immature, rash, but a good kid."

She relaxed. "He was really nice to me."

"Exactly. I have to go help." *With the bodies.* He left that last part out. "I'll be close."

"I love you." She held his gaze.

"I love you too."

He quickly fled the kitchen, already wanting to get back to her side, but he had to help his family. That was what made them such a strong pack.

Chapter Eleven

Charma was tired and more than a little disturbed at the number of werewolves who came into the kitchen in search of food. It was a shifter trait to get an appetite when they smelled meat cooking. It was *what* they were burning that made her queasy.

"I think that's the last of them." Dan started to put away the food. He was a nice kid in his teens. "I hope so, anyway. We're out of ham and turkey. The only thing left is bologna."

"Thank you for all your help."

"I'd do anything for Brand. He's cool."

She smiled, feeling a sense of pride. "He is an amazing man."

"He's kind of like a father to me. My old man was killed when I was a kid but Brand mentors me."

"He does?" She liked finding that out. Garrett wasn't a role model in the pride. Her ex-mate was the epitome of bad influences on the younger males.

"Oh yeah. There are a bunch of us without fathers and he teaches us stuff. We can't afford handymen coming out to our place so he'll drop by to show us how to fix whatever breaks, for free. We even go hunting together. He always tells us to leave the families alone."

Surprise tore through her. "What?"

"Animals. Not people." Dan laughed. "You should see your face. He gets pissed if we go after a momma with babies. That's what I mean. We're supposed to only take down the older stags and bears. The meat is tougher but he says it's good for us."

That was her Brand. He was a sweetheart. "I see."

"Werewolves don't kill humans. At least not in this pack. You have to have a damn good reason and it has to be approved by the alpha. They have to pose a serious danger to the pack." His gaze traveled over her. "We also apparently don't kill she-cats. Not that I'd hurt a woman. Brand taught us that there's nothing worse than being a bully. We're naturally stronger than most humans but even female shifters don't stand much of a chance in a fight against a male. He also lectures us about sex with humans, you know? Be gentle, don't growl, and reminds us to keep our skin. It would be real bad to burst into fur on top of one. They'd freak out."

The conversation had shifted to a topic she wasn't comfortable with. "I'm sure they would."

"I don't date humans. I mean, what's the point? I want honesty when I'm with someone. I'd have to lie to her about everything or risk her hating me for what I am. That would be the worst. The alpha would have to decide if she was a danger to the pack. My mom would also flip out. She wants grandkids who shift. It's a coin toss when you crossbreed." He frowned. "Shit. I wonder how weird your kids are going to turn out. I mean, will they look like you or Brand? How freaky would a half-kitten, half-pup be?"

227

His questions caused a stabbing sensation in her chest. She wasn't sure she'd even be able to get pregnant. She'd never met a she-cat who'd had a child with a werewolf. Her human half might help with that but it was uncertain. Would any possible children be shunned by the pack and deemed to be freaks? She knew all about not fitting in and being looked down upon. She wanted better for her children than she'd experienced as a half-breed.

"Enough," a deep voice growled, startling Charma. She'd been unaware of the person who'd walked into the kitchen behind her. Rave met her gaze before glaring at Dan.

"Go outside and do something useful."

"Brand told me to guard her. I mean, protect."

"I've got this," Rave announced. "Scat, pup."

The kid fled without another word. Charma faced Rave and forced a smile. "Are you hungry?"

"I already ate a rabbit." He wore sweats and nothing else. "I was feeling a little raw after all that fighting. That's a joke. You're supposed to laugh."

"I like my meat cooked."

"You don't shift, right?"

She shook her head. "No." She worried that Brand's cousin might have wanted to get her alone to warn her off. It would be understandable if he wasn't happy with his cousin's choice of mate.

228

It was a natural reaction to cross her arms over her chest to protect her belly and heart.

He noticed the gesture and both eyebrows rose. "Easy," he rasped. "You can relax. I'm cool with kittens, remember?"

"Yes." She fought her instincts and lowered her arms.

"Sorry about the pup. He was running off at the mouth but that's a kid for you. They're pretty thoughtless at times. He didn't mean to hurt your feelings."

"He didn't."

He just stared at her. He reminded her a lot of Brand and she could see the family resemblance. They had some of the same mannerisms — and that look stated that he wasn't buying it.

"Not much," she admitted.

"Brand won't give a shit if you birth him kittens or dolphins." A lazy grin surfaced on Rave's face. "He's crazy about you."

She hesitated. "What about the rest of the pack? Will any of our kids be in danger if we're able to even have any?"

"Never."

"How can you be sure?"

He chuckled. "Because we're the Harris Pack. Nobody fucks with us and lives. You're one of us now, Charma. You also won't be the only one who has mixed kids. My oldest half-human brother mated a human, and another one is mated to a quarter-puma. We're sturdy stock."

"I just want them to be healthy and happy."

A beep sounded and he reached inside the pocket of his sweats and removed a cell phone. He touched the screen. "Sorry to be rude but I need to respond to this text." His thumb tapped out a few words before he put it away. He glanced up at the ceiling, then back at Charma. "I had to tell her I'm alive. She was worried."

"Your mate?"

He masked his expression. "Someone I'm spending my heat with. I'll stay with you, though, until Brand comes in."

"I'll be fine. Go check on her. I take it that she's upstairs?"

"Yeah." Heat crept into his cheeks. "In my old bedroom. How embarrassing is that?"

"I don't understand."

"My parents never bothered to clear out the rooms and change them around. I still have all my teenage shit in there. I'd forgotten how many posters I had with nearly topless women straddling motorcycles until I walked her in there. Would you want Brand to see the room *you* grew up in?"

"Probably not. It's all pink and frilly. That was my mom's taste instead of mine. She was always decorating our rooms the way she wanted us to be."

He cocked his head.

"I was kind of a tomboy."

"Got it." He swept the room with his gaze. "How is the food supply holding? There's more in the freezer downstairs."

"Most have eaten. It's pretty dead right now." She regretted the words. "I mean—"

"Don't sweat it," he interrupted. "We have a sense of humor. Luckily we only lost two of the pack. How are you holding up?"

"Good."

He studied her shirt. "You fought?"

"One of your enforcers touched me and his hands were bloody."

"Brand is going to kill him."

"It wasn't in a bad way. He kind of put me in a closet to keep me safe."

His phone beeped again and he removed it, read the screen. He typed a response. "That's good. We don't need any more deaths today. Sorry. It's my brother."

"Braden?" She hoped he'd say yes.

"Yeah."

"Ask him how my sister is."

His head snapped up. "What?"

"He has my sister."

"Why?"

She sighed, telling him the facts she knew. Rave appeared grim as he typed. He paused, reading the response. "She's fine. Her ankle was twisted but that's about it. She said to tell you hi and she's okay."

Charma resisted the urge to lunge and tear the phone out of his hands. "May I talk to her?"

"Hang on." He texted something else and then the phone rang. He held it out. "Here you go."

Her hands trembled as she accepted it. "Bree?"

"I'm okay. Are you okay?"

"What the hell are you doing here?" Fear and worry raged at hearing her sister's voice.

"I thought the pride was tracking you. Garrett said you ran away. Did he hurt you again?"

"No. It's a long story. Are you hurt? Randy said his brother had you."

Her sister paused. "He's dead. Braden saved me." Her voice lowered. "He's a werewolf."

"I know. He's treating you okay?"

"Yeah. He packed my ankle with ice and we're hanging out in a basement. He said you mated his cousin. How is that possible? Is he lying to me?"

"No." Charma glanced at Rave. His gaze kept darting up at the ceiling. "Listen, now isn't the time to talk all this out. You stay with Braden and I'll be there as soon as it's safe."

"Okay."

"May I talk to him?"

"Sure. Love you."

"I love you too," Charma said, and waited for Braden to take the phone.

"Yes?"

"Please protect my sister."

"I will."

"And Braden?"

"Yes?"

"Don't touch her. Do you hear me?"

"I do."

"We'll be there as soon as it's safe to travel. Bye." She hung up and handed the phone to Rave. "Thank you. I was really worried. He'll keep her safe, won't he?"

"Yeah." He darted another glance at the ceiling.

"Go. I'm fine. You're worried about the woman upstairs. That's obvious."

He seemed unsure.

"I'm fine. Brand is right outside."

He strode away toward the living room. Charma watched him go and leaned against the counter. She closed her eyes. Things could have gone so much worse. Bree could have gotten hurt, or had a werewolf who hated cats find her instead of Braden. Brand could have died. Randy could have taken her away.

"Hey, cat."

The male voice drew her attention as she opened her eyes to stare at an unfamiliar werewolf. "What, wolf? You hungry? We only have bologna left to make sandwiches but I saw a box of corndogs in the freezer. They'd only take about a minute or two in the microwave."

He looked scary as his eyes narrowed. She guessed him to be in his sixties but shifters looked a lot younger than they really were. He directed an unfriendly glare her way and a sense of danger stabbed at her.

"I'm Charma, Brand's mate."

"I know who you are."

"Do you want a sandwich or corndogs?"

His nose flared. "Corndogs. I want six. I'm hungry."

She spun around. "I'm on it. Keep your pants on." She was grateful he wasn't naked. "Ketchup?"

The silence caused a chill to run up her spine and she realized she probably shouldn't have turned her back on him. It was too late though. She jerked open the freezer and removed the box then faced

234

him. He hadn't moved any closer, but he didn't appear any friendlier either.

"Mustard," he finally answered. "I'm Raymond Borl—and I don't trust your kind."

He got points with her for blunt honesty. "I don't blame you." She tore open the box and counted out the corndogs. "I'm not real fond of prides myself. I'm half human." She held his gaze. "Chips? There are some bags in that cupboard behind you if you want some."

He hesitated. "Just that." Long seconds ticked by. "Thank you."

"Thanks for not attacking me when you seemed to want to. Brand would be furious, and he's got a temper."

"No shit." The older man sat on a barstool at the counter. "All those boys are hotheads but they run a fair pack. I came from one that wasn't so hot."

She microwaved the corndogs. "Everyone deserves a fresh start somewhere."

"I guess they do."

They appraised each other and the older werewolf hunched in his chair. "Don't repeat this...but my joints are killing me." He flexed his fingers. "Is there any booze to be found? I could use a shot of whiskey or something to ease some of the pain."

Brand was prepared to tear Raymond's head off when he walked into the kitchen. He was too close to Charma, and he didn't like that one bit. He was glad he hadn't instantly reacted instead of waiting to hear some of their exchange. "There's a full bar downstairs. Hit it up when she hands you that food. I'm curious why you're here."

"I told you I didn't want to hear my son-by-mate nailing my daughter. He filled my basement with some of his friends to protect the house, so I came to fight."

"We appreciate that." Brand stood next to Charma, feeling better that she was within reach in case the cagey bastard decided to attack her.

"We're pack. I don't always agree with the decisions made but in the end, that's what it comes down to."

Brand removed the paper plate from the microwave and held it while he added mustard. "Here you go. You can't miss the bar. I suggest the whiskey."

Charma remained silent until they were alone. She stepped in front of him and lifted her chin. "How are you holding up?"

"Good." He didn't want to think about the tasks he'd just performed, one of them being cleaning up the mess in the attic. The carpet would need to be replaced. "Where's the pup?"

"Rave had a chore for him. I was fine. He heard from Braden and I got to talk to my sister. She's okay."

He was grateful. "I'm glad, hon. I hated you being so worried about her and stuck here. We'll be able to go home in a few hours. The carnage outside is mostly dealt with and the families of the deceased in our pack have been notified. Just don't go downstairs and open the big chest freezer. Both bodies were put in there until their families can collect them. We were lucky we didn't lose more."

Her expression almost made him laugh. "Their kin will want to bury them in the pack cemetery. It's not safe to travel yet until we make certain our territory is cleared of all pride. Some of them are severely injured and probably in hiding. The enforcers and a few of my cousins are tracking them. We only burned the pride members who died. I hope that doesn't offend you."

"No. Of course I hurt for their families, but only enforcers were sent for the joining. They know the risks. It's a sad fact of life that most of them don't have a long lifespan." She bit her lip, staring up at him.

"What is it?"

"Do you have to keep being an enforcer for your pack? I mean," she rushed on, "I know you'd always want to fight to defend your family but could you step down from the other duties?"

He liked that she worried about his safety. "I could."

"Your uncle wouldn't be angry?"

"Nope. He'd understand. Most do after we mate, unless we were born to it. Kane and Klax will always be enforcers. Those two are naturals."

She remembered the twins. "I'm glad they're on your side."

"Ours," he reminded her. "This is our pack. Why don't we head upstairs and shower? I know I could use one, and that dried blood on you is going to drive me insane."

She nodded. "I think I've fed almost everyone."

"They can fix something themselves if they show up." He held out his hand. "Just don't stare at the blood on the carpet up there. There's nothing I could do about it today. That's going to require ordering new, plus the pads. I'll come back in a few days to take care of it."

It was a reminder to both of them about Randy and how close he'd come to taking her away from Brand. She clasped his hand. "Lead the way."

The fighting had worn him out but not enough to dull his desire to get Charma naked. He locked the door once they were inside the attic, grateful for the privacy. The broken window had helped air out the stench of a recent kill but not by much. He was torn between the desire to just take her home and the need to remain at the alpha house for a few more hours. His dick decided, though, when his mate walked into the bathroom, stripping. The sight of her bare back was enough to make him groan.

238

She turned her head, meeting his gaze. "You coming?"

"Yeah. I plan to." He grinned, hurrying to join her.

She laughed. "You know that isn't what I meant. I was distracted but now…" Her nose flared. "You smell so good."

The sight of her fangs spurred him to tear off his pants and pin her against the wall once she'd stripped bare. He didn't care if they both had blood on them. He just wanted to kiss her.

"Water," she urged as he lifted her high enough to press his hips between the parted thighs she'd wrapped around him.

He groaned but turned, releasing her with one hand to yank open the shower door and step inside. She clung to him the entire time. It only took seconds to turn on the water and pin her against the tile. Warm water sluiced down their bodies. His mate found his lips, kissed him.

It took control not to just bury himself balls-deep in her. It quickly slipped away, though, when her nails dug into his shoulders, urging him on. He lifted her a little higher, pressed her back firmly against the tile and drove home.

Her pussy clamped around him. He growled and tore his mouth away from hers to avoid drawing blood. Her cries of pleasure assured him that he wasn't causing pain while he fucked her hard and deep.

The sharp stab of her fangs biting into the top of his shoulder sent him into the mother of all orgasms. He locked his knees to keep them both upright as he rode out her climax. Her muscles clenched and unclenched around his shaft, milking every drop of cum from him. He shook from the force of it.

"Wow," Charma panted.

Slowly coming down from the high, he nuzzled her throat and opened his mouth, his tongue tracing the column down to her shoulder. His fangs were out so he used them to gently nip her skin. She shivered in his arms and gasped. His dick had started to soften but it instantly hardened again, ready for another round.

"Mating heat," he rasped. "I'm not done with you."

"Good. Put me down though."

"No." He liked her exactly where she was — in his arms, pinned against the wall. He loved having her thighs wrapped around his hips. He lifted his head and stared into her eyes. "The heat has backed off enough to allow me to take my time, hon."

He started to move again, almost withdrew his cock completely, paused and then drove home, deep. Watching the way her eyes narrowed and her features twisted with ecstasy turned him on even more. Her fingernails kneaded his shoulders, a reminder of her leopard blood. She ran her tongue over her lips to wet them and moaned while he kept up the leisurely pace.

"Faster," she ordered.

"No. I want to enjoy watching your every expression this time."

"Bastard."

240

He laughed, knowing she didn't mean it. He'd missed playing with her. She'd snap soon, always did during her heat, and he couldn't wait. Charma was aggressive as hell and he kept teasing her until she hissed.

He tensed, believing he was prepared for what she'd do. He was wrong.

His old Charma would have bitten him again, urging his wolf to surface. Instead she used his shoulders to lift up suddenly, the slippery, wet tile against her back helping her dislodge his dick, and she bucked sharply. His feet slipped and he fell back but tried to protect her as they went down. Charma released his waist with her legs and his back hit the other side of the stall. He landed on his ass on the tile, with her coming down on top of his thighs.

He was stunned for a second but took note that he wasn't injured. Just his pride.

She laughed and rose, her hand reaching between them to grab the base of his shaft. She straddled his lap higher and adjusted his dick at the entrance of her pussy. She released him to grip one of his biceps and ground her hips down, taking every inch of him.

He didn't even mind when she wrapped her other hand around the back of his neck, getting a good hold on his hair, and began to frantically ride him. It felt too good to do anything but enjoy it. He watched her face when she tipped her head back, seemingly oblivious to the water that rained down on them.

Brand gripped her hips, helping her move on him faster, and used his feet against the opposite wall to brace so they didn't slide around. He glanced between them, loving the way her breasts bounced. He wanted to catch one of her nipples with his mouth but he couldn't dip his head enough with her fisting his hair. White-hot bliss seared through him as he started coming again when she did.

"Brand!" she yelled and slumped against him. Her grip on his hair eased.

He adjusted his hold, hugging her tightly while they recovered.

"Did I hurt you?" She kept her face down, resting it against his chest.

"Never. Do I have any hair left?"

"Sorry." She laughed though.

"Liar."

"You were just out there fighting so don't bitch about a little hair tugging."

"How about being body slammed in the shower? I think the drain is going to leave an imprint in my left ass cheek."

She laughed harder. "I hit my knees on the way down so we can compare bruises later."

His hands slid down from her hips to cup her ass and he squeezed. "Are you hurt?"

She raised her chin and grinned at him. "It hurts so good."

He sobered, staring into her eyes. "Damn, I missed you."

242

Her mood changed from playful to serious. "I'd rather die than live without you."

"Me too. We agree. Only neither of us is allowed to die. We have a lot of time to catch up on."

"It's a deal."

Epilogue

Four weeks later

Charma paced the living room, glancing at the clock for the hundredth time in half an hour. She had to trust that Brand would be home for dinner. She'd said it would be ready at five o'clock. She glanced again at the time. He had less than twenty minutes before the pot roast came out of the oven.

"Calm down," Bree ordered. "They're going to walk through that door at any second."

"We haven't heard anything." That made her afraid.

"They didn't want anyone tracing their whereabouts. You know that. That's why they left their cell phones at home. The last thing the Harris Pack needs is another war with the pride council."

"They could have bought one of those disposable cell phones."

"They didn't want any incoming calls on this line from that area. Come on, Charma. You know all this. It's going to be fine. Have some faith."

She blew out a frustrated breath. "I wish I could have talked him out of this. It was insane."

"He's got all his cousins with him. They insisted on going, and he's got the twin enforcers too. They scare the crap out of me every time they look my way."

That distracted Charma enough to stop pacing and stare at her baby sister. "Are you happy living with werewolves? No one treats you bad, do they?"

Bree scoffed. "Not more than once. I ran down to Rave's bike shop yesterday to drop off something I found at the alpha house that belongs to him, and one of his employees made a rude comment. Rave grabbed him by the scruff of his neck and made him kiss the counter." She winced. "That's what *he* called it, but the guy lost a few teeth. I was assured they'd grow back but it was brutal. Rave offered them to me to make a necklace. I said no thanks. Werewolves are more aggressive than leopards."

"What did the guy say to you?"

Bree smiled. "I think he's been punished enough. I'm not going to tell you. You'll get angry and tell Brand. He's already on the hunt for one male. I made Rave swear not to repeat it to anyone. I was afraid Braden and his other brothers would go after the guy too. He'd lose more than a few teeth for those crude comments."

It was a reminder that Brand wasn't home and she glanced at the clock.

"It's going to be fine," Bree murmured. "You don't see *me* freaking out."

"You're younger and can't imagine all the horrible things that I'm picturing. I remember when you used to think Garrett was hot. He is *so* not."

Her sister winced. "That's an understatement if Brand gets his way."

"I asked him to rethink this."

The front door opened and Charma spun, raking her gaze over Brand as he entered the room. She flinched at the sight of a fresh wound near his temple but he otherwise looked okay. She rushed forward and leapt, her arms wrapping around his shoulders.

"You're home!"

"Always." He hugged her, pulling her farther up in his arms. "We Harrises kicked ass and nobody on our side was hurt."

They were moving, and she realized he'd carried her down the hallway and kicked the new bedroom door closed, giving them privacy. She lifted her head, staring into his eyes. "Is it done and over with?"

"Yeah. The bastard is dead. I killed him myself."

"Good."

He studied her. "You okay?"

She nodded. "I'm just so happy that you're alive and home." Her gaze flicked to the wound on his face. "Are you hurt anywhere else?"

"Just some bruises and a few claw marks. He wasn't a good fighter. I'm almost depressed over how easy that son of a bitch was to kill. I kept in skin so they'll think a human killed him when they find his body."

"What about scent?" She didn't want to offend him. She thought he smelled wonderful, but even her half-shifter side could detect he was a werewolf. A full-blooded one had better sense of smell.

"He's taking a bath in the river near where the pride lands end. They won't pick up anything off him by the time he's found."

"Are your cousins okay?"

"They didn't have to fight at all. They just watched my back when I took on Garrett. You'll never have to worry about him coming after you."

"I told you he wouldn't bother."

"I don't believe that for a second. The guy had an ego, and there's a good chance he'd have heard about where you ended up one day. Shifters tend to talk about a wolf and she-cat mating. His pals would have teased him until he wanted payback. I just made damn sure he's never a threat."

She couldn't deny that Garrett might have wanted revenge if he discovered that she'd left him for someone else. The fact that Brand was a werewolf would have really set off his temper. "I can't believe he was alone when you found him."

He cleared his throat and glanced away.

"What?"

He met her suspicious stare. "Um, I might have had a little help with that."

"I don't understand."

"I called your sister Meg and talked to her mate. He wasn't a fan of Garrett's. I like Cole. He's a pretty cool guy for being a pussy."

"You involved them?" That surprised her.

"I told Cole what Garrett had done to you and how I wanted to make sure you were safe. I needed to get your ex alone without his entourage."

"What did Cole do?"

He hesitated.

"What did he do, Brand? Did he put himself and Meg in danger?"

"No. He just kind of implied that Bree had come back and she was hiding out by the river. He mentioned that she didn't feel safe coming home, after finding out Percy had told Randy he could have her after her coming-out party."

Her eyes widened. "Why would Garrett want to see Bree? I keep telling you, he had to have felt relieved when I ran away. He sure as hell wouldn't want me to return to the pride by trying to learn from her where I'd gone."

Anger deepened Brand's voice. "He wanted you because of your looks and because you could breed him litters. Meg was taken—and you have to admit that Bree looks a hell of a lot like you. He's suddenly single. Think about it."

248

She did, and it turned her stomach. "Bree never would have agreed to mating him. Never. He had to know that."

"You didn't agree either but he forced the matter." He moved them to the bed and shifted her a little so he could sit.

She straddled his lap. "I'm glad he's dead."

"Me too."

"Did you tell him we mated?"

Brand grinned. "Your scent was all over me. I didn't have to. He was shocked at first when he ran into a werewolf in his territory, but then he inhaled. It was priceless, seeing his expression right before I decked him. I made sure he knew why he was going to die."

"I really don't want to hear the details."

He nodded. "It was faster than I'd planned but I was pissed. He started telling me how I'd regret mating you, and why."

She could imagine, remembering what he'd said about her to the enforcers that day in his father's office. "You're sure you're not hurt?" She sniffed and picked up slight traces of blood but none of it was fresh. His clothes were new, since she didn't pick up Garrett's scent or that of the laundry detergent they used. They had that right-out-of-the-store smell.

"I'm great, hon. It's over. They'll find him floating in the river. We covered our tracks. A jerk like him had to have made a shitload of enemies so it will be a long list of suspects. Shifter law is on our side anyway. He was a danger to my mate."

She still fretted, not wanting to bring another war to their pack.

He seemed to read her mind. "We handled them the first time around and I doubt they'll want to come back. Just a few of them survived, and it was only because we allowed it in order to send a message to your council."

"Percy is pretty vindictive, especially when it comes to his oldest son."

"He sent most of his toughest enforcers here to fight. They died. He can't be that stupid."

She wasn't convinced Percy could be sensible when he was angry, but she kept silent.

"We'll deal with whatever happens."

"I just hope this doesn't blow back on Cole or Meg."

"We thought of that. All Cole has to do is play dumb by claiming that's the information he had. It's not as if Bree is ever going back there, now that she's become part of our pack. Cole also seemed pretty certain that Percy wouldn't dare attack his pride."

"Darbin would kill him. I think I told you that's Cole's dad."

"I met him. He's cool."

"You met Darbin? Why?"

Brand hesitated. "Your parents and brother moved into his pride with Meg, after they realized you weren't coming back. I

250

assumed you'd like to have access to them when you miss your family."

"Yes."

"We talked and decided we'd meet up halfway, in neutral territory. We'll send a few pack to protect you and Bree, he'll send a few pride to protect your family, and we've worked out a treaty between our people. We're no longer enemies with Darbin's pride."

Charma felt a little overwhelmed by her mate's thoughtfulness. "Thank you."

"I don't want you to have to give up the rest of your family to be with me." He hesitated. "You're going to really want them around in the coming months."

She frowned. "What does that mean?"

His hands cupped her hips and he leaned back a little, glancing at her stomach. "Your scent has changed."

She blinked a few times, trying to make sense of what he was saying.

"You're pregnant, hon."

She gaped at him, stunned.

"You are." He grinned. "We're going to have a baby."

"But..."

"I'm sure. I had my cousins take a whiff of you a few days ago when we were at the alpha house. It's not just wishful thinking on my part. You went into heat, I was already in heat, and jackpot." He chuckled. "We're expanding our family."

Her heart pounded with excitement. Tears filled her eyes but she blinked them back. She reached down and touched her stomach in wonder. She'd always dreamed about children with Brand.

He covered her hand with his. She looked up into his eyes.

"You are," he repeated. "We're going to be parents. We just need to get our doctor to schedule you an ultrasound soon to find out if we have enough bedrooms or if I have to build an addition on the house before they're born. We'll want all of them sleeping on the same floor as we are." He winked. "You might be carrying more than one."

"You think so?" She'd always known it was a real possibility to get pregnant with a small litter.

"I hope so, but I'm going to worry until you give birth." His grin faded. "That's why I took care of Garrett today. No way in hell was he going to get a chance to harm you again."

A new thought struck. She bit her lip, pondering if she should say anything.

"What is it?" He arched an eyebrow. "I know you too well. What's on your mind?"

"What do you think they'll look like? Do you worry about that?"

"I hope, if we have any girls, that they look like you. That's a given."

She laughed. "You know what I mean."

"It doesn't matter. They are ours, hon. Chances are they'll be able to shift. You're half and I'm full-blooded. I know they'll be as cute as hell, whatever a part-wolf, part-leopard looks like in fur. It's also a given that, in skin, they'll look like every other kid." He paused. "It'll work out."

"I'm so happy but I'm a little scared."

"The pack will accept them. They'll never be snubbed or teased. No one would dare. I'd kick their asses."

He did know her too well. She let go of her fears. "Okay."

"I'm kind of a badass," he teased.

"You are." Her gaze lowered to his chest. "And you're really sexy."

"I think we should celebrate by getting naked."

"You always suggest that, and I agree."

Brand leaned closer until their noses touched and stared deeply into her eyes. "We're together and the world is right. Relax, Charma. It's all uphill from here. We've been through the worst when we were apart. Nothing we ever face could be as bad as life was without you."

"That's very true."

The playful glint returned to his gaze. "I want you to know that you saved me when you came home. Someone was offering me up to their grandmother as a boy toy. She wanted to become a cougar. I much prefer belonging to a sexy leopard."

Her eyebrows rose.

"Seriously. Do you think I would have made some grandma a happy woman?"

She reached for the buttons on his shirt. "Let's find out in about twenty-five or thirty years when our kids start having babies. I'll be a grandma then."

"I can't wait. I'll embarrass our grandkids by chasing you around and carry you off to bed every chance I get."

Charma choked up and hugged Brand. "I don't know what I'd do without you."

He held her tightly. "You're never going to have to find out."

Made in the USA
Columbia, SC
24 May 2022